NO-MAD

PABLO REIG MENDOZA

To Mrs. Marta.
"It has to be done!"

No-mad

1 Euro-babel

Juan Mari Arzak, the renowned Basque chef, once said that the best dish in the world is undoubtedly the *croque-madame* sandwich made with special care. What at first glance may seem like a "boutade", from certain angles, it becomes a Templar truth. Throughout my short existence, some characters who were fond of trying the same dish in every restaurant in the world had gained in-depth knowledge on the subject, and even today, they can still correct some great chefs' hands.

I was especially impressed by a couple, he a prestigious journalist and she a psychologist now separated by those twists and turns of life, who had been studying the famous Waldorf salad for ten years. Against all odds, he was able to make an exquisite version with his own hands. It's something that can be said of very few wannabe gastronomes, who have tried everything but cannot execute a scrambled egg, nor a fried egg since the latter's good preparation requires basic knowledge of thermodynamics.

Another prominent figure of the Spanish Transition, also a journalist, has been tasting every Asturian *fabada* on sale on the face of our planet. I do not want to imagine the displeasure to which such a singular purpose will have led him, not because of the proverbial heaviness of this regional dish, but because this admired friend has traveled a lot. There are cooks out there who deserve to be beaten.

In this frantic beginning of the millennium, the occasional emigrant, especially the new generations, are in the habit of killing the *saudade* of their mother country by opening some canned specialty. In Spain's case, the Litoral *fabada*, a national icon, takes the palm without competition. The French are more inclined towards *cassoulet* and the Maghrebis towards *couscous*. I don't want to mention all the world's peoples at this point so as not to prostitute the argument, but God will recognize his own. In passing, I will limit myself to comment that the brownest Italians are only satisfied with sauces since it is a country of delicious starters and execrable main courses. Saxon peoples are still a step away from refining their taste; "the Renaissance has not passed through here", as another friend settled in London for a long time would say. Other lights the Saxons have, but not this one.

The fact is that with the aforementioned canned *fabada* it happens like with fast-food hamburgers. The first spoonful takes you directly to your grandmother's arms in the case of *fabada*, as does the first bite of the *dirt-mac* at New York's Fifth Avenue, even if you have never set foot on it. In this way, as you go along, the fabada turns into a disgusting paste with the tempered paprika, and the American sandwich confesses its undeniable resemblance to cardboard, both in taste and texture. Whoever speaks from the authority of a promiscuous life will be able to observe the astonishing resemblance of this gustatory effect with the memory of many of his fleeting lovers.

Each of us, therefore, to a greater or lesser extent, has a few dishes that we try throughout our lives, and we form a judgment of how, for example, the immortal archetype of the *croque-madame* sandwich should be. So far, in my case, the best is undoubtedly the one from the *Casa da Guia* pastry shop in Cascais: dry-toasted village bread, a brush of warm butter, and an unbeatable Atlantic Ocean. There is another problem of gastronomy as a major art. It is very difficult, if not impossible, to reproduce the same sensation twice.

Egg Benedict itself marks you in many ways depending on one's mood, the place, the company, and the surroundings. So one tries to remember the soft curves, the fine hair, and Anne's sidelong complicit glances that morning at the Hotel du Louvre having oysters with brioche and Billecart-Salmon for breakfast.... they never taste the same to me since then. What's more, ever since Anne stood me up with a "good riddance" and then her lawyers let me know about our son's visitation schedule for the next ten years, in the few "old times" relapses we've had, Anne doesn't taste the same to me either. I guess it's mutual. The truth is that I have never again accompanied oysters with brioche.

Is this text you're reading a novel? I don't know. Somehow I am committed to writing in the first person in front of a PC screen, just as you are committed to letting yourself be carried away by these lines. Words have an extraordinary power. Now that hypnosis has been renamed NLP, and everyone seems to be able to lecture on the subjects of suggestion, the power of body language, and other animals, few have noticed the birth of *a priori* suspicion in social and professional relationships. Let me explain: raising an eyebrow for your interlocutors is enough for them to wonder if you are creating an anchor of influence to implant a mental virus in them. They don't know you usually raise your eyebrow three hundred and fifty-four times a day, simply because you have the tic and because you can do it, with both eyebrows. While they think of defending themselves from your underhand attack, they miss what you wanted to tell them, even if the latter was not worth much either.

I have started this text talking about the *croque-madame* sandwich for the simple reason that we are at the beginning of the rant, and I am at the beginning of the day. In all the good households I know, the day begins with a more or less copious breakfast. So, for the sake of good vibes, I beg you to lower your defenses. You are not going to be hypnotized while reading this text to the end. I do not have ten mythology notebooks that will activate your cultural triggers for you to go out to the street to ask your government to do something so that absolutely nothing happens. I intend to share a stretch of the road and make it fun for both of us, me writing and you reading. I have finished my breakfast and can start the day with a bang; it begins in a borrowed apartment in front of Via Fatebenefratelli in Milan and will surely end with some emotions.

For a few weeks now, Jérôme has been organizing a party for the newspaper he runs, and it's a themed party on a budget. As it is the anniversary of the illustrious newspaper's founding, they have rented the Vittorio Emanuele gallery's great crossing for a few hours. They are going to bring an international personality representative of each section who will give a short talk. Closing a public space for a party was almost unfeasible, so Jérôme - from now on Jéjé, as he is familiarly known - managed to apply for a filming license at the town hall. I must say that Jéjé is admirable in his ease of affectionate cajoling. He is Belgian but could be Totó's distant nephew and moves around Italy like one more of them. Not only has he convinced them that the shoot is for a Paramount blockbuster, but he has managed to get a fee waiver so that the daughter of a friend of the prime minister receives a few minutes of tape. *Tangentopoli.*

Jéjé and I met young and poor, which is the only real way to enjoy the European continent without being a millionaire, a tourist, or a pensioner. We coincided in an obscure office in Bonn, doing telemarketing for several multinationals. It was not easy, back then, to invade the privacy of homes to work the minds of housewives, and the cell phone was still a luxury available to few. On second thought, housewives still existed, and mortgages longer than ten years were a metaphysical impossibility.

I will not confess my age, but for what it's worth, in Germany, they still circulated hard and heavy German Marks. I always wonder why the coins were not square... The fact is that we made friends, and our friendship lasts until today. I guess it's because of intermittency, which gives time to miss each other and have juicy things to tell in further encounters. We were poor to the point of boredom then. Our meager savings were for drinking, but that did not prevent us from making lavish feasts of *risotto* with mushroom powder soup or pasta with grated *bratwurst*, not to mention the evenings of vegetarian *sauerkraut*. He was already announcing his journalistic vocation to the four winds, and I was beginning my dalliances with business psychology.

Before Bonn, Jéjé had made his debut in Rome as personal assistant to a die-hard politician, one of those who will never win an election. He was the first to talk about the legalization of drugs by setting an example, getting himself arrested for selling marijuana loudly in the Piazza Espagna. There is always something to learn from others. From all that Jéjé learned from such a commendable gentleman, the following comment was engraved in my mind: "The only reason for public service is to create difficulty to sell ease". I was recently reminded of this pearl when, in the queue of a ministry, I heard a Russian civil servant respond to the story of a hairy case: "Did he manage to make the whole thing up?" It is not the civil servant, it's the function.

So we met about a month ago in Paris. He was finalizing the details of a report on the latest student conflicts, and I had to give some assertive reorientation seminars in an American film distribution company. We met at about five o'clock in the afternoon at *Le Trappiste*, for the sake of tasting some abbey malts. It had been about a year since we had seen each other. He showed up on time, as usual. As always in his case, precisely at half past five because, according to him, half an hour late was the perfect compromise between the time that women who know how to assert themselves are usually late, and the usual British punctuality. I confirm that I have never seen or heard of a delay of less than fifteen minutes in the greater London area for those who have never waited for a train in the English Isles.

–Leonardo! *Comment ça va, mon petit père?* - he looked sincerely excited as he shook the water off his black raincoat. It was raining outside in that uncomfortable rain of the Aprils in this city.

–Great Jéjé! Nice to see you around these parts, balder and fatter! I reckon you still don't have time to take care of yourself. I saw you arrive by car and I ordered you a Lambic. Sit down and tell me the latest.

He instinctively reached a hand to the thinning blond locks that still lined his forehead as if to make sure of their presence. He took a seat shakily and planted a thumb on my glasses to return the "compliment". I just left the glasses on the table, and we both burst out laughing. His laugh is very characteristic, somewhere between the whine of a horny ferret and the victory cry of a turkey that manages to survive Christmas. A burst of contagious and exuberant laughter that never goes unnoticed and that, in the past, even cost us some nasty tavern brawls.

–Leo, Leo, Leo, Leo, *petit père*, you're not bald, you're not bald, but you're no thinner than last time. I come conveniently overexcited. In France, being a student and protesting always go hand in hand, and this time they have burned fifteen cars in the *Bois de Boulogne.*

–Fifteen cars! But don't the guys know about the displeasure of the owner, who is just another taxpayer? Even if the insurance pays, it seems nonsense to me. In Spain, public furniture has always been violated, with a particular preference for containers.

–No, *mon cher ibère*, insurance no longer pays in these cases, at least in the metropolitan area, since one law firm filed an appeal to qualify street protests as acts of terrorism. Another law firm, I think from the same owner, added to the dossier an argument on how student protests should be considered a natural disaster because university belongs to the city's ecosystem. The issue has been blocked in *cour d'assises* for three years because of some death that had nothing to do with the burned car. Car owners are in deep shit.

–I don't even want to know if you're pulling my leg or you're serious, you old savage. How is Silvia? That woman deserves heaven three times over for putting up with you for so long.

Jéjé took a long drink and pulled out his proverbial little packet of Drum, which he started buying in Bonn to stop smoking cigarettes, relying on his disgust for rolling tobacco, which he has not let go of to this day. I ordered another round while he answered me.

–Silvia deserves heaven, and I'm doing everything I can to make sure she earns it so that I have someone to intercede for me. The last one is that she wants to get married, you know? The thing is, I love her as I've never loved anyone and, if we didn't live in Italy, I wouldn't ask many questions, but her family makes me shudder. They are too Catholic.

–Too Catholic? How come? You are the son of a Marists's real estate contractor, with all the comfort involved. - I interrupted him - Besides, what is the yardstick for being too much or not enough Catholic, Jewish, Buddhist, or whatever? - He burst out laughing again and solemnly opened his glazed clear eyes.

Do you remember her sister's psychological pregnancy, for which I was unjustly made the main suspect? Well, many years later, in front of the firing squad, sorry, in front of the whole family at a dinner in Rome, they made me a philosophical trap remembering the incident, and I almost didn't make it. One is too catholic when one uses morality as a weapon against one's neighbor. God is love, *et point final.* But we were talking about Silvia. I wouldn't know how to live without her, and while you will see her at the party in Milan, you will both discuss doctrine and, by the way, practice your Italian. Order something salty, *je t'en prie*, and tell me what brings you to Paris, you tendentious punk!

—I'm coming out of an assertive reorientation seminar on Avenue Montaigne. Middle management is a tough nut to crack. I'm almost later than you, so the round of questions has been stretched out. - Another laugh à la Jéjé.

—Assertive reorientation? What are you inventing now, *mon petit père*? The butter-cutting thread or the hiccup-removing thong?

—We are like your law firms, we have a *coaching* team that teaches assertiveness in large companies, and I am part of the *SWAT* team that leads it. With that, we manage to keep the perfect mental balance of their teams. You know that multinationals' turnover is accelerating lately, and that creates imbalances.

–This year will not end without me dedicating a special issue of our weekly magazine to you, *mon petit père.* Do you bill what you bill for this crap you are telling me?

I always have a hard time explaining the nature of my work to a layman. It is usually a layman who signs the estimates, so I live in a permanent conflict between this personal difficulty and my billing objectives. Fortunately, it has been a few years since sales are closed by others, and I limit myself to giving my eclectic talks between planes, but that does not free me from having to justify my services on some occasions, and I have a reasonably well-defined speech.

–It's not that simple, you little fool! Your profession still has a creative component that serves to heal your neurosis, even though you make a living from selling advertising and politics rather than selling newspapers. Notwithstanding your cynicism, I know you care about keeping an editorial line that brings freshness to your readers, so you also end up resembling me in your function as an escape valve, but not in the other ones. In most professions, this is far from being the case. It is a matter of remembering that, even if business means numbers, those who go to meetings and run the day-to-day are human beings whose good performance also affects the profit and loss account. In an environment of global budget cuts, my job is to keep the troops' morale at acceptable levels and optimize groups and individuals' psychosocial lubrication. This does not make me Dietrich going to see the Marines, Doctor Caligari, or Charlie Rivel. Still, I try to ensure that my interlocutors learn to be like Houdini and strengthen their mental health without negatively affecting the company and their colleagues. Get it now, mussel graveyard with fries?

—You indeed remind me of many law firms with your description, and they certainly don't do badly either. All the more reason for you to have that space to explain your market to my readers. They also laughed at Columbus's egg and Brel's teeth. Seafood or *steak tartare, mon cher ibère?*

And so, between the ferret and the turkey, we finished our beers and went to review the always delicious meats of *La Maison de l'Aubrac* and its regional wines. The night lasted until the wee hours at the *Folies Pigalle*. It was a fairly well-balanced VA session, which we were told about by Martine, Philippe's wife, while we had dinner, and Jéjé gave me the details of the party's organization in Milan.

"Dear friend,

On the twentieth anniversary of *Giornale del Mondo,* we are pleased to invite you to the party's shooting that will take place at the Galleria Vittorio Emanuele, access Duomo, on May 29th, from 22:30 and up until the Carabinieri Corps kicks us out.

For the occasion, several personalities will delight us with a brief talk. We have asked them to develop an imaginary news item without each one extending more than fifteen minutes. Anyone who wants to be bored can come to our editorial office any day after closing time, but the party is designed to leave you with an unforgettable memory.

We count on your presence. Etiquette, good disposition, and a taste for quality music and surprises are requested.

Jérôme Van der Linden - Director".

We landed last night in Malpensa because of fog which, according to the captain, forced us to divert. I am accompanied by Sandra, a friend from Sao Paulo that I met in Florianopolis on a business trip and is now temporarily based in Oviedo. I should clarify that it's instead me accompanying her because Sandra is a beautiful brunette who is a head taller than me in sandals, and with whom, for my luck or misfortune, there has never been more than friendship.

Sandra is one of those sparkling people who guarantee good humor and no bitterness as long as you don't remind her of some chapters of her troubled past. Born Wanderleia in a poor slum of São Paulo, she had her name changed when she married her first husband, an obscure businessman from Minas Gerais. Sandra-Wanderleia had the head and good fortune to be able to attend university. She quickly found the opportunity to leave the *mineiro* in the lurch when his umpteenth mistress offered her a job while gossiping about her relationship with the man.

Today, the gentleman lives hooked to a catheter for life due to a Levitra overdose. According to Sandra, that's practically impossible, and she suspects a much more banal origin of the disease. In my opinion, her current name suits her better, just like her closet: always discreet no matter how bright and colorful. When I talk about her to third parties, I can't help remembering that impression. Sandra is a woman of color, a fresh breeze on this often ashen continent.

–O Leo, is this Malpensa in Milan or Venice? I can't stand so many cabs anymore! As Jobim used to say: *Brazil is shit, but it's good; while the first world is good, but it's shit.*

–Don't overreact, Wandi. Besides, you will soon understand that this is part of the hype. You'll see, my dear, you'll love it.

–You call me Wandi once again, and I'll give myself to you to see you fall in love and never touch me again! And if someone finds out, it will be worse. I should never have told you. Always Sandra, bullocks!

My spoken Portuguese is quite good, but we have an agreement to speak in Spanish to learn as much as possible during her stay. Since I also believe that Portuguese-Spanish hybridization will soon be the official language south of the Rio Grande and the Pyrenees, I don't think it's a bad idea to start practicing. Besides, the poor girl is having some problems with Bable there in Oviedo. I find it very funny when she attributes the origin of the dialect to the Asturcon horses. She speaks excellent English if you can call English what they speak in the United States. As a London comedian said in his Dublin performance: "You must be surprised by my accent. It's normal. I don't have any. I'm British, and that's how my language sounds." We also have a frictionless friendship agreement; we like each other too much to spoil it all over a few hot cramps.

–I apologize a thousand times. It won't happen again, Wandra.

–Son of a bitch...

The apartment is impeccable. It was a penthouse with high ceilings, quite decadent, and spectacular bathrooms, bathtubs, and lots of mosaics. Sometimes, it is justified that the Italians call apartment houses *palazzo*, although it can be misleading, as misleading is the amount of "princes" who swarm these geographies. Jérôme lent it to us as a special favor. I told him he needn't to, since I had managed to get paid for a talk in the local offices of the same company we were working with at that moment in Paris, and he must surely be up to his ears in commitments due to the organization of the party. Jéjé left no option for further discussion: he invoked the ferret and the *petit père* and hung me on my nose. We took possession of our rooms, and I gave Sandra her set of keys.

–If you flirt, discuss, or get lost, this is the address. Please, if you pick up, make sure he's not into group sex. I don't feel like arguing with a hundred-plus-pound buck at six o'clock in the morning in hostile territory.

–If you want to patronize, you bring your son. Besides, I know how to defend myself, don't you? Oh, and that doesn't stop you from being a gentleman: you make breakfast.

–Wandra...

–*Filho da puta...*

–They'll be the best breakfasts of your life, even if I'm a flirt too, I'll tell you that. Make yourself comfortable. I'm going to sleep. It's going to be a long day. Do you like your room?

–I love it, and you know it, fool. Shall we take a bath together and turn off the deal one night?

–Don't provoke me. Maybe you like it too, and I don't feel getting at the party with the memory of your skin. Women notice that right away, and you know I'm looking for a formal girlfriend. Ask me again the day after tomorrow, and we'll be even.

–Hahaha! No chance, handsome. I'll check the bookshelves. Good night, go. Kiss.

This deal is the scariest challenge I have set for myself in the last ten years. Luckily, we've been training to flirt for a long time now. If nothing has happened in all this time, it's a sign that we've reached cruising speed in the relationship. I like Sandra, and her Paulista accent with those Britishized R's brings back memories. If someday we stop these verbal games, it will be a severe warning that one of us has fallen in love, then we'll see.

My talk starts at ten o'clock in the morning, and I'm pretty well on time. I have already checked my emails, nothing worth mentioning. Thanks to this contract and the expense notes from the last trip to Buenos Aires, the bank is also smooth. I turn on the HK in the living room and play at considerable volume and in replay mode a version of *Tico-Tico no fubá*, by Baremboin, a delight. I leave Sandra the steaming breakfast on her bedside table with my raincoat on, a reversible Aquascutum electric blue and matte yellow, almost tattered but still in shape and more traveled than Willy Fog. Some garments are as evocative as the eggy mix-and-match on the tray.

–Up, girl! If it gets cold, it's you to blame. Then you go to bed again if you want. Anyway, you'll end up going to the living room when the *Tico-Tico* drills your brain - sleepy and disheveled, Sandra is equally colorful.

–Motherf... Eiiii! What a lovely smell! Thank you, *amôr*. Today, I won't insult you anymore. Have a nice day. Call me when you're free, and God bless you. I'm meeting Pietro, that Sardinian friend I told you about. We'll probably spend the morning shopping.

–If this Pietro wants to, invite him to the party. We'll figure it out with Jéjé. It's black tie, don't forget. *Beijinho*.

–Mrrrphr, okay - she yawned – Go ahead, go. Thanks for the coffee.

A fine mist has taken hold of Lombardy. I go down the stairs thinking about the benefits of digital tools. *Replay* and *random* are two elements that didn't exist in vinyl times, and being unimportant details, they have always given me play. *Replay* allows turning any song into a mantra. Until Rio de Janeiro's carnival, I had always judged mantras as the apex of redundancy, although it proves useful for some therapies. The same *samba* for an hour and a half (samba music there is spoken in masculine and danced in the feminine) with a trained audience radically changed my point of view, and some emblematic songs I ingest in this way, discovering new things.

Random has already become inseparable for that game of luck that allows matching the songs' meanings coming out with the thoughts arising in the subconscious and the things that are happening around. There is even morbid anxiety at the end of each song to see how clever the algorithm gets for the choice of the next one, just like adspotting on the Internet.

My client's offices are in a downtown building covered entirely by a marquee with a fashion advertisement. It's like a Christo intervention subsidized by a third party. Few cities lend themselves so well as Milan to this kind of visual exercise, mostly because if there's one thing the Italians know about, it's style. I don't think any brand would leave a poorly designed stencil in the sight of such a punctilious public. According to her golden pin, Sofia Ferrara leads me to the conference room with an angry and sweet dalliance while I am sorting out my ideas for the talk.

I will reuse the Buenos Aires presentation on "Archetypes and Workflow", so I have the topic chewed. I will present in English, as it is the house's official language, and my Italian is very rusty, largely due to the Portuguese I have been practicing lately. I wish vulgate would come back for everyone. From Portuguese, I especially like the construction and its sixteenth-century sound. The Lusophones people still make good manners and respect the norm, but their language does not pass the years. There is a tense debate these days in Portugal's university about the last reform of the road code of words, on the other hand inevitable, I think. *"O Leonardo está a prestar atenção?"* The third person's use as second and those non-gerunds move my spirit with the same grace as their users maintaining elegance in walking in a hard fight against gravity and rain. The heels and the Portuguese cobblestones, common to the sidewalks of all the countries of the old commercial empire of the pot-bellied naos: fire and tow.

The audience is arriving in the hall. The coffee smell in the adjoining foyer is dissipating, and I have everything ready. I distract myself by reading the day's newspapers on my laptop. I always completely disconnect from the subject matter in the minutes before a presentation. This produces unexpected results, and I end up stringing together new ideas on the fly, almost without realizing it. The main headline of the *Giornale del Mondo*, whose website I had never accessed before, catches my eye:

"A VOTE COSTS 20 EURO IN CAMPANIA".

How much will a plate of *ossobuco* under the Lazio region cost in old Liras, I wonder? No mention on the front page of tonight's party. Lights out.

2 Euro-babble

The projector shows a Rorschach stain. It's the first one. I use it a lot to thread the argument, whatever the subject to be covered. I never manage to see anything other than an extended Venetian mask in it, but I've never told anyone that.

"Good morning to all of you. My name is Leonardo Ruiz, and we have the whole morning to go over some business psychology together. As you know, the title of the talk is *Archetypes and Workflow*, and it is not trivial. Your company has just spent an undetermined amount of more than a couple of million Euros to implement a *workflow* pilot system for project management in Europe, of which mine has only a few thousand left to scratch. Notwithstanding our bonhomie when it comes to budgeting, I will endeavor to share some added value since the purely functional part is already covered by the software developers with whom we have a *joint-venture*."

"What you see behind me is one of the famous Rorschach blots. I don't want you to worry about interpreting it. I don't want to know how many of you see a bat, nor am I going to ask you today about your relationship with your father or whether you look down before you flush. The issue at hand goes more to the side of Jung than Freud's. That stain is there to make you aware that, although computing is about ones and zeros put in a certain order. We all live to take a slice of that flow of money that is business, there is a psychological component that, if we know it better and use it to our advantage, can make our task easier and avoid us some future annoyances."

"In this psychological component that I mention, the main actors are you, system users. You are in charge of feeding the system, detecting errors, interpreting the workflow, and transmitting information internally and externally. You, in short, are the human factor, and if your abstraction capacity is low or is altered, the system suffers globally. Each failure or deviation of one is a little garbage that dirties the good end of the whole."

"I also know that many of you were involved in the definition of the tool at the time, so it is also partly the result of your know-how. You know that it is a pilot and, as far as I am concerned, this means purely and simply that it is an unfinished tool. At some point, it will stop being called a pilot, but this is pure formalism. It will never stop being a pilot because it is more of a process than a tool. It will never be finished because it will never stop changing and correcting itself following your business's behavior, and it will be a faithful reflection of the good use you make of it. Not only of the tool but above all of what it manages: the projects in progress."

"So, we see in the next slide two definitions. A *workflow* is an automated process that links project information (tasks, activity, departments, etc.) to reduce workloads and trace the occurrences of those projects."

"An *archetype* is a model or example of ideas or knowledge from which many others are derived. It models thoughts and attitudes proper to each individual, to each set, to each society, even to each system."

"My department has chosen a set of common working archetypes: the first ten major arcana of the tarot, and related them to the ten key elements of the life of a project. With this association, we will analyze the company's pulse and detect behaviors and project forecasts. In short, we are going to map the psyche of the company over time and, by using the tarot instead of colors or another formal set of archetypes, we will be able to match other behavioral databases from certain universities that are not worth mentioning."

At this point, I always pause briefly to enjoy the audience's shocked faces and whispers. The room is quite dark, but it is clear that no one is distracted. It's tricky at first glance to mix such seemingly disparate concepts as tarot decks and project management. It's even harder not to squirm in your chair when you think your year-end bonus may come to depend on whether the pope card or the death card comes out. In reality, it is a very powerful classification and monitoring tool. In the highest decision-making spheres, they know that there has never been a king or emperor in history who did not consult the augurs before a battle, but that is another discourse.

"Don't be scared by the tarot. There is no fortune teller in the human resources department, and if there is, she is not registered as a user of the tool. If you want to know a little more about the subject, do study some Systems Theory. At the end of the document on your desks are some references you can use for this purpose."

"In the following slides, we are going to go through those ten charts and establish the psychology inherent in their associated process. It is also not about you learning it by heart if you are not going to be part of the management team. Don't forget that this is ancillary and only useful for large volumes of historical data. Your primary focus should be on the practical operation of the tool, but, in the future, these studies will indeed mark key turning points in improving your processes."

"The fool. The fool has no numbering because he is mobile. In the classic tarot, the fool represents the man who travels through all the deck stations, and, in our analogy, the fool is, no offense, the user: you. In a way, you should feel rather honored since the fool is the central axis of our system. The most elusive and the one to be treated with the most affection. Capable of giving the greatest positive differential and, if not suitably combined, the greatest cost. For calculation purposes, its value is zero, and it is a zero that derives in two types of interpretations. When added to another arcana, it does not detract from its intrinsic value and has a wildcard effect. In the end, it is the one that executes and is present in every task and process. Simultaneously, if we use its multiplier effect, we can develop Boolean matrices and know that not enough skilled labor is being attributed in the data cloud. Not to mention its psychological value, which is the crux of the analysis at hand, the fool is always represented with a dog biting his clothes, and he doesn't seem to realize it. The dog in our system is the pressure of change. If the attribution of personnel to projects is fully optimized and, despite this, the business model shows no signs of improving, you have to act on the dog."

"The magician. The magician has value number one. The magician and the rest of the arcana take the values corresponding to their respective cards. We use the mathematical qualities of each of them to apply algorithms and combinatorics to perform our mappings. In the case of number one, it is its multiplier effect that does not detract from the intrinsic value of the card with which it joins, while it advances a step if we use it as a sum. So, the magician is the timeline. Each day in the timeline contains a magician. All the other active cards are spread over it, just like the objects on the table in the image, this being their psychological value. Suppose we have a thousand fools to consult 365 magicians, besides being able to start working the binary code mathematically. In that case, we only have to put into action the tools to turn the wheel during the fiscal year. These fools also have weekends, vacations, families. Similarly, a single magician can do more or less magic as a day can have peaks in turnover. Don't force the mess or get esoteric on your own. You could blow a logical edifice already well thought out. Do not forget that the model is as valid with tarot as with any other set of archetypes. You will understand that we do not have time to dwell on many details for each of the cards if we want to get to the lunch that has been reserved for us in Bergamo without getting our polenta spat out. Please take note of your doubts for the round of questions and answers while I continue the enumeration. Ah! I warn you that I am forbidden by medical prescription to do work talk during lunch, but I will gladly answer your emails if anything is left unaddressed during the meeting."

The rest of the talk went smoothly. I have it very well studied, and this is the presentation that I like the most. I understand that it is because of the use of tarot. In other disciplines such as assertiveness, teamwork, or specialization, I always have some laggards, but this one flows wonderfully. *Workflow* is a great product that is getting excellent results. I usually manage not to get interrupted until the empress, which is three, the last of the primes in a row and the one representing the project's business rules. Up to that point, concepts are clear: number two makes all its associates into peers, whether they are peers or not, etc.

I had a math teacher who used 1024 to calculate for almost every problem he demonstrated on the blackboard. It took me half a year to realize the subtlety of 1024, which corresponds to two raised to the power of ten, and whose understanding helped me accelerate my performance in class. I try very hard not to gesticulate during lectures. In this one more than the rest, mostly because of the tarot. I am working hard to avoid the eyebrow effect because I like to make sure that the message gets through and any fussing causes the audience to lose focus on the core of the issue.

At my suggestion, we had *Trattoria da Ornella* closed for us. We take a bus and then get on the funicular. As I am sitting down, I hear my name being called from behind.

–Leonardo! - I turn around and see Marco Sanzone, the general manager. As he gestures for me to come and sit next to him, I jump up in surprise.

–I was making you in France, or so Jean-Marc told me last month when you booked this trip for us.

–Right, right. That was the plan. I wanted to stay an extra week, so I could see you alone and, while we're at it, to pay you all for the polenta. I would like to know why you always end up in the same restaurant every time you come here.

–The day you find a better rabbit polenta, I will surely change my preferences. Until then, you know, I stick to my list.

I'm lying through my teeth, and you can probably tell. It's not that it's not the best rabbit polenta I know, which it is, but *Ornella* was one of the mythical stops on our honeymoon, and it's becoming one of the very few things that still tastes the same to me as the Anne of those times.

–If you say it is so, it must be so. How long will you stay?

–I'm staying for three days. I'm going tonight to a party at the Vittorio Emanuele, the Giornale del Mondo's twentieth anniversary, are you going?

–Surely yes, the crème de la crème will be there, so it must be possible to combine the useful with the pleasant. Anyway, we don't leave the *trattoria* without having a little chat, you and me. Because you want to collect soon the bill I have on my table, right?

–If it weren't for Coppola and Julio's ways, I wouldn't have crossed the Alps. You sure know how to talk to a man! Don't let it be too much. I have to pick up my tuxedo from the dry cleaner's. How's business?

–Well, you know, we are in crisis. I am fifty-four years old, and here we have always been in crisis. Crisis here, crisis there. Meanwhile, our sector is the one that suffers the most from piracy. We can't think of any more ideas to realign the business in other niches - he scratched his forehead with some disdain - the few we have tried are blocked by Jean-Marc because, according to him, they are out of the focus of corporate policy. Bah! Same as always, BS. Anything to add?

–You know my policy, Marco. Criticism must always be destructive because constructive criticism is consulting, and that has to be billed. With all my love, without passing on your budget, I reserve the right to remain silent.

–You like aphorisms more than a Roman. That phrase is from a Spaniard, the same one who called your King Juan Carlos I "the brief" - I am not surprised by his quickness - You consultants think that the rest of us only read *Topolino*. Well, here's one from a fox of the Apennines: More runs the greyhound than the mastiff, but if the road is long, more runs the mastiff than the greyhound.

–Yes, and if the road is too long, neither the mastiff nor the greyhound will get there, only the hound. If you want to blame piracy for your misfortunes, blame the telecommunications companies, who are the owners of the tube through which everything is filtered. But of course, for that, you have to have what you have to have.

—I'd love to throw my ferret imitation at him, but the bill is on his desk, and he looks well disposed, better to stick around.

He was right, a polenta out of this world. The funny thing is that it is a dish that I hated as a child, although it is also true that, outside this place, I order it very rarely. Marco kept asking for negronis for everyone while they were bringing the appetizers. I stopped at the second one because it is an explosive cocktail, strictly speaking, one of the most dangerous. If you don't have a good palate, the first sip tastes like lightning, too strong and bitter. The traditional one is equal parts Campari, red Martini, and gin with a few orange peel slices.

I have a friend in Madrid who reduces it with a prosecco tip and transforms the devil into an imp. But here in Bergamo, on the wooden table where they were going to serve the polenta in the traditional style, and with the perspective of the night ahead, it would have been imprudent to get carried away. I don't mean by this that I disdain the ethyl trip of the negroni. On the contrary, before realizing it, you drink five, and when you wake up, you become the czar of all Russias. If I am not mistaken, it is the only hangover that does not wait for the next day. After three hours, you are on the verge of a stroke.

—What a polenta, my goodness! I'll have to bring the kid when he lives with his dad. My son's name is Luis, and if his mother doesn't hurry up, I'll be the one to make him a little brother. Despite Cain and Abel, it is good to have siblings. I have two, Laura and Jorge, both younger than me and much more warlike. I have never quite understood why nobody says Abel and Cain if it is the alphabetical order. It must be because Abel died without descendants, and being an end of his race, he is biblically put last. The wine is from Sicily and has a good mouth presence. *Cusumano* it's called. The Lombards are learning to get out of the two Bes... Barolo-Barbaresco, Barbaresco-Barolo and always at Burgundy prices. Everything evolves, is destroyed, and some rare exceptions remain frozen in time, like this *trattoria* or the tobacconist of Pedraza de la Sierra in Segovia.

–Well, *Leonardetto*. They've all gone to see the village. Let's order some coffee, and you'll tell me about the project. I've been talking to the guys from Argentina, and it seems that your tarot invention has left them quite impressed. Positively, I mean. They even warned me to give my employees a chastity guardian.

–A chastity guardian? What do you mean by that? - I'm still with half my mind riding on the cloud of the abundant feast.

–They told me that if we let you loose, the boys would leave the meeting ready to visit the Prime Minister's castle in their underwear if necessary. Since Tiberius and Caligula, we Italians take those things at face value. On the other hand, I have been able to verify that you have left them quite convinced, which speaks a lot in your favor. I'm curious. Who approved the tarot? Jean-Marc didn't, did he?

–The thing was negotiated in Los Angeles - I've already come down from the cloud. Marco wants to get something out of me that he knows I'm not going to tell him.

–I will go straight to the point. Those ten arcana are the friendly side. What about the other twelve? And don't give me evasions. None of us are sucking our fingers here. Are they going to take away our analysis power and keep it only for themselves?

–Hey, Marco. I don't know if it's the Negronis, the 2012 effect, or the Vatican's proximity, but you seem a bit mystical now with the arcana! This is not *The Sorcerer's Apprentice*. It's more like *Alice*, and there are no wonders, only DVDs. I lead the project in that part, and I'm like Pythagoras. I only see numbers. Don't make any wild guess, or you'll screw it up for me. It's enough of a commitment to have chosen tarot. Besides, you are not the only clients who have bought the tool, you know? For your peace of mind, I will tell you that yes, next year you will have the budget of the other twelve on your desk, and it will be a little more expensive, but much better - Marco leaned back slightly in his chair but visibly relieved and smiled again.

–You see how right I was? - he said triumphantly, - so there is already a signed specification booklet with the 22 complete arcana at the head office. When will you show it to me?

–You know very well that this is confidential, and I'm gambling with the project, Marco. I have confirmed it to you by word of mouth only because, as you say, it falls under its weight, and that does not compromise me - now I am relieved. - You only have to wait twelve months, one per arcane, if you want to stay in mysticism.

–Well, I'll wait, but I had to try. You understand, don't you? And don't worry about the twelve, your secret is safe with me.

–Thank you, if you keep that B-movie tone, I'll play the *Dracula* soundtrack on your cell phone.

We said goodbye with big hugs and some jokes. He's a good guy, Marco, and a great professional. He has seen it all and has always managed to keep his nose out of the water. I am a little uncomfortable with the arcana subject, not because I didn't expect something like this to happen to me at some point because of the tarot, people want to dream, but because he was not out of tune in his appreciation of the mystical part. The Los Angeles specification booklet has been signed to analyze the corporation based on the 22 major arcana and the 56 minor arcana. Indeed, the enormous power of analysis that the minor arcana will provide will not leave the United States.

I feel doubly guilty because our company has not hired any cabalists or seers. Still, we have our MIT engineers team who will integrate the solution by putting together all our clients' models: a mathematical and functional cloud that will leave Internet search engines in diapers. The tarot comes from the book of Thoth, but it will take at least ten years for aggregated data to make sense in front of the Egyptian pantheon, and what interests me is the little brother for Luis and tonight's party, which could well come together at the same time and place. It is almost four o'clock in the afternoon. Let's see what Sandra does.

–Hi, babe! I've already left, and I'm arriving downtown. There is quite a traffic jam. Where are you going?

–Hello, fool! We are at Duomo square. You can't imagine the setup here. Are you coming?

–I was thinking of going for a swim, but come on, meet me at the front door in fifteen minutes.

3 Euro-bible

Europe is also a vast field of churches and cathedrals. In my constant search for intimate pastimes, it occurs to me that if the great pyramid of Cheops has about two million and some granite blocks... How many more cathedrals could we build by dismantling it? At some point in the evolution of our time's recycling fever, someone could execute such an aberration. Who wanted to stop him would only have to argue the Ottomans' dismantlement of the white stones layer or the origin of the stones of the cathedral of Cuzco. One of many examples that the old is usually the layer that supports the present.

Mohammed showed in this a very peculiar practical sense: Islam, besides killing the devil with a stroke of a pen, only needs a single stone to create a planetary cult. Christianity has had a more invasive and multiplying effect on the physical plane. Because of the buildings and because if we put together every "authentic" nail of Christ revered all over, we would surely get enough iron to make a replica of the Golden Gate.

I love cathedrals. I find them fantastic places to relax the spirit and distract oneself by searching among their various symbols. Some time ago, I came to the following conclusion: trying to embrace the whole is complicated. Worse. Its discovery leads unfailingly to nihilism, as in the mathematics of zero and infinity. In the end, what is distracting is to enjoy the path in the very little that we manage to embrace and get drunk with the beauty of simple things and details. There is also infinity between any two points, no matter how close they are.

Whenever I go to Paris, I tend to visit or revisit one of these stone books, and the last visit was no exception. Passing through *Les Halles*, I entered *Saint Eustache*. In Spain, this saint is the patron saint of hunters, and I find the analogy with the homonym we carry in our ears ingenious. One of these days, I will check if there is a Saint Fallopian in the saints' calendar.

As I entered the church from the side, after a quick pint of red ale at the adjacent Irish pub, I was startled by the imposing sound of a Zen concert taking place. "Now that's syncretism!" I thought. I stood there, enraptured for a long hour, listening to the gongs. It was intense to see the church organ mute's rods, surprised by this invasion of its Asian competitor installed on the altar. Feeling the exoticism of the reverberation in the vaults made me travel far away.

My favorite cathedral is Notre-Dame, without any specific reason, because they all have their message. In Duomo's case, its shape reminds me suspiciously of a wedding cake, but I like its interior and its color. What I don't like at all is the intense population of pigeons in its square: those infectious flying rats that populate cities. The local photographers have a curious custom. They throw bread crumbs on you and take your Tippi Hendren's extravaganza picture in *The Birds*. I knew of a girl who had to be attended by the emergency services, as she suffered from an atavistic fear of those particular birds.

I see Sandra and Pietro waiting for me in the left column. There are two other women with them that I don't know yet. Pietro is just as Sandra had described him to me: an Eric Clapton look-alike, but back at Woodstock and, like all the locals, elegant even with the rags he wears. In some cases, they pay a million dollars for the same rags at Armani, and it takes them half an hour to make them up before they go out on the street. It is true that sometimes, I have done the same. The two new ones are quite good-looking—a brunette and a blonde, as in the blonde and the brunette's zarzuela. The four of them are speaking English.

–Ciao young people! I am now a free man, and I don't know for how long - all turn their heads in unison.

–Hello, cat! - Sandra comes up to me and applies an unaccustomed, fleeting kiss on my snout. I rightly suspect she nurtures an interest in Eric Clapton rather than music. I say rightly because of the look on Eric's face and the Brazilian pinch I get on my ribs - Come and meet some friends. This is Pietro, and these are Lucia and Chloé.

Curiously, Chloé is the brunette and Lucia the blonde. I shake hands with Pietro with my second best smile, which is no less sincere, and two kisses on the cheeks to each of them, this time with the best smile in my repertoire. Chloé hesitates, looking for a third kiss, so she is French. Lucia gives me the opposite cheek, ergo Italian, also owner and mistress of green eyes to lose sense. She won't see my pupils, but my eyes always give me away.

–Well, finally, - says Pietro. - We were afraid that the traffic jam would keep you at least half an hour longer. In Milan, traffic jams are proverbial. Sandra tells me that you are a business psychologist. I'm very interested. I own a shoe factory, and I can exchange good ideas for limited series shoes if they are outstanding. The shoes are irreproachable. I'm sure you will find your weakness.

–Hehehehe! The irreproachability of my ideas is not bad either, and they are also limited series! We'll square that better right away with some cappuccinos. I like your friend, Sandra. And you, beautiful girls? The question is always horrifying, but what do you do for a living? How do you know these two elements?

–I am from Enna, in Sicily, and I live here, - Lucia added to her green eyes with a velvet voice. - I was the girlfriend of this mameluco until I discovered his defects. The three of us studied together, here in Milan, and my father still sells leather to this cretin, so I'm forced to see him every time he buys. Just kidding, today we get along quite well.

–I came to see Lucia. I work in Lyon for the Ministry of Culture. We manage the subsidies for European cinema. Hey Sandra, you haven't told us what you do!

–I'm on a sabbatical year in Oviedo. I still don't know if I'll last the whole year.

Chloé is more beautiful overall than Lucia, at least to my taste. I have an instinctive fear of

French women. Like that of the girl with the pigeons, it must be atavistic because I have no reason for it objectively. Even, and I find it commendable, only in France have I seen ultra-feminine women changing their car's wheel on their own. It probably has something to do with the cliché of the *précieuses*. In other words, sexist nonsense.

–Sandra, you are unfair to the Asturians, - I told her. - You have arrived at the end of winter, and you haven't had time to get to know them well. If I find the time, I'll come up there one day and show you the little I know. While I'm at it, I'll teach you how to eat seafood, which is only good on the Cantabrian coast. One wonders why you Brazilians have seven thousand kilometers of coastline. Is anyone else going to join us tonight? If so, I have to tell Jérôme right away.

–If Sandra lets me, I'm going on that Asturian trip too.- now she's pinching me again, triumphantly and much more painfully.

–I'm sure you're not going without a partner, are you, Leo?

–I've canceled a dinner today so I can go with you both, girls. What do you say?

Chloé, snorting French-style and looking up alternately at the sky and Lucia's face, remains silent. Good move, Pietro. I'm missing something because they take longer than usual to respond as if they are communicating with each other mentally. Finally, Lucia takes the initiative.

–Chloé is very tired and will stay at home, but I'll be happy to come with you, don't you mind? - This last one staring at me. That's it. I'm hooked. With those eyes, there is no possible defense.

–It will be my pleasure, - I answer as I, ipso facto, dial the ferret's number. Something tells me that green look is hiding something else, and I want to know what.

When I dial the number, I am well aware that it will be busy non-stop. I step back a bit, so they don't hear the maneuver. I leave a message on the answering machine that I know he will read. Only then, I notice the vast tent covering the access to the event site, and the number of trucks and cranes let into the square. I have a good feeling. Sandra surprises me from behind.

–Chloé and I are going with you to see the inside of the Duomo, and the ex-lovers will pick out some party clothes for Lucia. We have an hour and then will meet at the Brera art gallery for coffee next door. Are you going to make sure the Italian girl isn't into group sex before you invite her to our *palazzo*, pig? It looks like we won't have to wait until tonight for either of us to get a plan.

–I don't know why you say that - I reply dismissively. - Besides, Chloé is a few meters away, and she can hear you. If you want to be indiscreet, say it in Portuguese. But ok, the Italian lady has turned on a light bulb for me. It's been a long time since I've warmed up with just light bulbs, should I? And the next kiss you steal from me, you'll find my tongue. You've been warned.

–Whatever, Don Juan. Let's go to church. If you kneel, you will have to pray.

I signal to Chloé, and we enter the Duomo. It's starting to get a bit chilly in the square. It's a bit windy, and it's a huge open space. There is no beggar at the door. How strange. Sandra's face is a poem.

–A-W-E-S-O-M-E! Did you already know this place, Chloé?

–I have to admit, even though I've been living here for the MBA for a year, I've never been inside. Not bad. Don't let my apparent lack of enthusiasm fool you, but I have entered more churches than Abbé Pierre because of my profession. I can't be surprised anymore, although I agree with Leo. I also like it better on the inside.

–I don't know who Pierre is, but this is spectacular! What columns, what a floor, what an organ! I'm going to light a candle. It never hurts. I'll give you one, Leo, for any outstanding accounts you may have. You too, beautiful! I'll be right back.

–So, Chloé, you know many churches? I find you to be of few words if you don't mind my saying.

–Yes, I am. You're not wrong. It's not your fault. I'm also quite suspicious of men, although you seem less wolfish than average.

–I'll take that as a compliment. It must be psychology. We usually inspire confidence in people who need to talk and distrust in those who have something to hide.

–Hehehe, just like decent priests - it's the first time I've seen her smile -. You must be good at what you do. Maybe I do need to talk. I know many churches because I was a novice for a few years, and my tutor was very itinerant. My boyfriend died in a mountain accident, and my parents thought it would be the best way out after several unsuccessful treatments with your colleagues.

That comment about the priests tastes bittersweet to me. Even so, there is some truth in what Chloé says. Nowadays, the couch has replaced the confessional. On many occasions, I come across cases of people who desperately need advice and do not know how to cope with it because it is seen as a symptom of weakness. Some overcome this fear and ask for my card and address. As I have never consulted privately, I usually take their details and personally arrange for a colleague to contact them.

I copied this referral form from a colleague I met at the Anna Freud Center, in London, during seminars on schizophrenia. He taught me many things in that short period that are still useful to me. His golden rule was never to treat acquaintances, and sometimes he found it difficult to avoid commitment. On the other hand, he was crazy. He walked around town at all hours with his cat hooked on his shoulder, like Long John Silver's parrot, and he was a vegetarian on even days and some key dates depending on the phases of the moon. He was full of manias that he consciously cultivated, and he spoke very little. On one occasion, he explained:

"Leonard, our business is a priesthood and consists ninety-nine percent of listening. Church people indulge with impunity in speaking to marriage partners, and then it's up to us to clean those unhappy people out of their frustrations built up over decades. We cannot afford the same mistake if we want to get them out of the hole and prevent their dysfunctions from spreading to the next generation. So we must strive to cultivate degrees of insanity by funambulating that dangerous line ourselves. To never cross it completely, you have to do as alchemists do with the atanor: get your hands dirty and put degrees of sanity in each leak. *Solve et coagula*, and observe everything from a distance, from behind, so as not to inhale the mercury smoke that would make you cross the line."

"Your ally is time. Years are a sum of moments. Be crazy in the instants and wise in the whole. Externalize both as little as possible and never stop studying. It is only over when it's over. Don't forget that we don't know which side of the asylum wall the real madmen are on. Our abode is the wall." Michael is his name, quite a character. We still congratulate each other on Christmas. I catch myself strolling at ease with Chloé for quite a while now under the vaults of the Duomo and discussing religion in an eavesdropping attitude.

–How are you doing with God after the coping?

–I am more concerned about how God deals with me, but I have learned not to believe in a man with a beard and not suspect that free will is only given to us to blame us later. Today, I think that God is the sum of all. Dogma says a lot of nonsense, and that's why I didn't stay. What's the point of me locking myself behind habits if I can be useful to others out here? Why should I refuse to have children if I ovulate every month? Don't I ovulate by his holy will? I don't question myself anymore, I have reached an acceptable balance, and I think I am happy that way. Then there is the original sin.

–On the original sin thing, we could sit in front of the bonfire for a few weeks. But no pun intended, Chloé. Although the Lord has given you beauty, I can't keep quiet about that.

–You are very kind. Listen, I'm an ex-nun, but I'm still a woman, French, and working in the motion picture industry. Don't think I'm a prude, either! - second smile of the day, I give it back to her.

–I'm sorry, it slipped my mind. Carry on with the original sin, please.

–The story of Genesis reeks of machismo from every pore! It is an abject trickery that leaves women in an awful place and has caused many barbarities. Long before there were religions, our societies were matriarchal, and look what the world has become with your patriarchy! I am not a feminist. We are not equal, and it's better that way, but neither inferior nor superior. We owe it to ourselves to be complementary, and that would bring down many barriers. The war of sexes makes us worse than animals. On the other hand, I do not believe that sin consists of distinguishing good and evil. I suspect that our greatest sin is the pride in judging God and his creation, which is where we are.

Here I have to swallow my answer, especially since we seem to be starting to get along. There is a logic in her discourse, but I find the point of patriarchy quite annoying. I am rather convinced that the current state of affairs is an exceptionally well-orchestrated hidden matriarchy. I once read about a group of women during the French Revolution who argued their right to power with a resounding "We're not receiving orders from mindless men we've carried in our bellies!" The bull rarely sees the bullfighter, who is the one who moves the cape. For me, Eve's sin is to have managed to delegate to Adam's drone the function of worker and monopolize the queen's role for herself without Adam's knowledge. The result of exacerbated feminism, which is nothing more than renowned suffragism, is that they are once again workers, but they also have epidurals. I do not know if they have won with the change.

–I agree with your argument of complementarity. Without a war of the sexes, we would all be much happier.

A voice with a thick German accent squeaked from behind us. We both gasped.

–Ach! In this country, when you don't say "*Porco governo!*" you say "*¡Puta Eva!*"

The clarification comes from a bearded redhead whose rags certainly did not come from Armani and has not seen a shower for a few days. Showering and motivation are similar. They have to be exercised daily, because their effects don't last long. To his left is Sandra.

–Hello people! This kind gentleman has been explaining to me the history of the cathedral and its works of art. Didn't you miss me? I wanted to thank him with more than coins. Do you have ten Euros, Leo?

–It's been a long time for three candles, - Chloé replied, holding out a bill to Sandra. - We were distracted talking about God at his home.

–*Gott in Himmel!* Ten *DeutscheMark!* Nobody has been so generous to me in, let's see... - he puts a finger to his temple, mumbling - at least three months! Let me introduce myself, gentlemen. I am Wolfram, nothing to do with Mozart. He was the wolf of the road, and I am the wolf-crow. Everyone here calls me Fritz, and I have been the Duomo's beggar for so long that I can hardly remember. If this were Paris, I would indeed have a hump. Fortunately, my painful sciatica is punishment enough, it seems - he crosses himself.

The man has overtaken Lopez-Ibor on the right for quite some time. His wandering gaze betrays him. His eyes turn entirely around the celestial vault in a completely involuntary way in five-second lapses and always from left to right. His association of ideas seems coherent, and his fixed beggar status indicates he should not be dangerous. I let myself be carried away by his provocation.

–There are no more Marks, my friend. Now it's Euros; we are gathering Europe.

–Hahahaha! Europe, you say, Europe... He's another one of those who think the war is over! It's spelled Euro, but it's pronounced *"Deutsche Mark"* and regulated in Germany. This time, we are winning. Don't you see? It has been enough for us to tolerate that others do not appreciate our sauerkraut, to spread everywhere like ink. The Nazis are but a drop in the ocean. Two thousand years to get here! All we lack is selfish England and the Russian bear, as usual. Although the bear is already softening - at this last, he smiles, showing us his deplorable dentition. Chloé stirs with a particularly cautious and mischievous look.

–Whenever you jump the Maginot, there will be *résistance*, gentlemen. And Americans.

–But you will always be our best allies! Your Côte d'Azur is our invention, and we are back! Go to Saint-Tropez, if you have any doubts. And we don't care anymore if you pronounce *beemdublevé*, as long as you buy our *wünderbar* cars. Your governments know what's right for you, anyway. The cowboys keep their oil and go and steal it from their neighbor, not us. You ask us for a wheat factory, and we make you see that, if with wheat, which is using 20 of water and 80 of grain, you also make beer, which uses 20 of grain and 80 of water, you will come out ahead. We sell you the wheat factory, finance you the beer factory, and keep the exclusive rights to both spare parts and maintenance. Ultimately, we drink the beer when we come to see you to make sure that you have enough money and our computer scientists design the business's control with our software... enough for everyone! Thus paying all the taxes!

It seems that the madman is not so crazy. Although he has warmed up, he is still talking to us. I'm beginning to suspect that, rather than Lopez-Ibor, the Teutonic energumen has overtaken Dabrowski on the right. The three of us are in one piece.

—You were talking about Genesis, all the first-born sons of my family have been men of science. I am a theoretical physicist, quite retired as far as you can see. It happens that there is no longer a border between science and faith, so I choose the cathedral! We already knew this in the academies, but thanks to the Internet, information spreads, and the academies die. It is true that, in the process, the original data gets quite dirty, but the basis is pure and unshakable no matter how much it is vulgarized. I give you a banal example: Einstein came to us with relativity and the speed of light. We were already more or less clear about the photon, and the wave-particle dichotomy made us dream. Now everyone wants to unify the sciences in a single formula, while the New Age arrogantly insists on involving the observer in quantum physics. *Ach*!

Religions have been pounding on the solution for centuries! But by disguising it as the Nibelung, we did not pay any attention to it. All forces are the same with different velocities and degrees of concentration: light, magnetism, electricity, etc. What has clouded our understanding is to rule out a priori that these forces have their consciousness, and that the infinite cloud of forces is God. God has endless fun putting his tentacles of energy in every corner of matter, and we will never understand him because he limits our point of view. Does the cell of your knee know that your wife does not like the smell of pizza? Time is only a point of view, you think you are moving, but all you have been and will be is eternally fixed. Our genetic spiral is nothing more than a bit of complexity over the first photosynthesis: light pulls the mud and plays with it. I need a blackboard the size of the world to begin to express this in formulas. God does not happen. God is! Today, yesterday, and tomorrow! For Him, time is incongruity and weakness! - His tone begins to reverberate off the walls - I am God playing Wolfram! You are God playing yourselves! When you remember who you are, the game is over! When the game is over, you will remember who you are! God doesn't play dice! He is dice! Eternity is too dull! It takes peaks and valleys!

–Is this gentleman bothering you? Fritz, if you do your thing again today, you'll sleep well cooled down.

The *carabiniere*, who is two heads ahead of me, puts a hand on Wolfram's shoulder. He is the first uniformed man I have ever seen in my life with a ponytail falling behind his cap, a rather comical cap, by the way. The volume of the guy's biceps leads to fewer jokes. Our madman curls up in open submission.

–No, officer, excuse me. I was trying to explain to these tourists that I am a Protestant shepherd. Since I lost my flock, I have not stopped complaining.

At this, Wolfram squirms like a crocodile and, with a violent yank on the ponytail, knocks the lawman's cap off his head. With amazing skill, and in less time than it takes to think about it, he twirls the man's neck with the ponytail forcing him to the ground. Almost simultaneously, he grabs the ten Euro bill from Sandra's hand with his left hand, while with his right hand, he rubs her breast as a bonus for the metaphysical speech with an added audience.

–A thousand thanks, miss! As there is no generous woman, I steal love in the square - are the lyrics of one of Lucio Dalla's best songs.

He runs down the stairs of a wooden pulpit while the carabiniere joins in to chase him by blowing his whistle.

–It is possible to live in a very intense situation without participating in it! - he exclaims loudly from the pulpit.   - His voice booms like Moses' - *Ach*, go on sleeping! If I had been Adam, I'd pull out the snake's fangs and wear it as a condom!

The agent is almost catching up with him on the stairs. With one leap, he leaps from the pulpit like a deer and flees in terror down the central aisle, laughing loudly. In a quick assessment, his pursuer decides not to take the plunge and returns down the stairs, exiting through a side door while rhythmically blowing his whistle. The expression of astonishment of the visitors of the Duomo is as in a hidden camera show. Ours should not be less. After endless seconds, the three of us burst out laughing.

As we head for the exit, I take in the German's speech and remember Michael and his parrot-cat's method. In the next Christmas card, I will tell him the story of the wolf-crow. I will probably look for Wolfram another time I pass through Milan. Then I will bring a notepad. I knew of a similar case who once decided he had to make up for his lost time and spent three years walking backwards. It took him three years to relearn how to walk properly.

We have a few extra minutes to stop by the stores in Corso Vittorio Emanuele. Pietro has confirmed a small delay in choosing the perfect color for Lucia's dress. The Fiorucci store enchants Chloé. If Raphael were to raise his head and check his angels' revenue, he would surely be satisfied and would not stop claiming his *royalties*.

In between stores, Sandra tells us the story of *Aleijadinho*, a one-armed sculptor to whom practically all the carvings in Brazilian churches, especially in the Ouro Preto area, are attributed. Sandra acknowledges that there is a fine line between myth and historical figures. That does not detract in the least from the beauty of his carvings and, if one is guided by the number of Niemeyer designs that have been erected in the architect's long life, perhaps full credit can be given to the one-armed man's story.

4 Euro-bubble

–We won't have time to see either Caravaggio or Mantegna, Sandra. Whose idea was it to have coffee here? Fortunately, we're close to home.

–The idea was mine - Pietro answers - and it is not original. I borrowed it years ago from an Indian supplier, and it has worked very well for me. It turns out that most of us disdain the excellent work of secondary coffee shops and thus miss out on some wonders. You'll see their *cappuccino*. It's not just the product itself. It's the environment, people... There should be a guide to these things, but there is not. It's just another form of lateral thinking. My mother, whenever her bladder betrays her on the street, the first thing she looks for is a five-star hotel. What do you say, Chloé?

–It's not a bad idea. Sometimes, in Lyon, I also meet at the train station without getting on the train. I have a weakness for a Lebanese-owned pastry shop. Only there I manage to order both a traditional *croissant* and pistachio puff pastry for breakfast. You won't believe what we just went through in the Duomo!

–Pietro is right. In Madrid, if you overcome your initial reluctance to pay the Círculo de Bellas Artes entrance fee, you can enjoy a cafeteria that is a real showcase in the middle of Antonio López's painting. Indeed, they have long since replaced their comfortable sofas with wooden chairs, but it is still worth it. You don't have to have a bedroom to enjoy the Palace Hotel's rotunda or its restaurants, although the latter are best explored if you go with a subsidy, it's still the Palace. - Lucia's radiant eyes are still in place. Sandra gives me an accomplice wink that happily no one sees.

–Aren't you going to show us your purchase, Lucia? - she says.

–It's a surprise, you'll see it tonight, but it's spectacular—a beautiful *bustier*. I'm going to hate to wear it.

–Ah! In Spain, we call the *bustier "palabra de honor" (word of honor)*. We still don't know if it was the tailor who gave his word to the lady that it was not going to fall or if, on the contrary, the lady herself spent the whole evening with her hand over her heart to hold it in place.

−We call it *tomara-que-caia*. Look how the story changes - Sandra answers.

−What does *tomara-que-caia* mean? - asks Chloé.

−"I hope it falls" - I translate. They almost all spill their coffee on each other.

As if it were the most natural thing to do, the sexes' war is subtly redefined in the small space where we are. The girls form a huddle, showing each other their purchases and telling Lucia about the German beggar adventure, and the two of us start talking business.

−Well, Leo. Let me tell you about my problems and see if I can get something out of you. For my part, I have already sent you the private catalog by email. With or without an idea, I insist that you choose the model you like the most. It's my gift for the party.

−Thank you very much, Pietro. I won't stop doing it. First of all, tell me, you mentioned an Indian supplier, do you buy leather in India?

−Yes, few pieces, but they give a good game with some models. In the end, sacred cows die, too, don't they? I am joking. Besides that, it is imperative in the current context to make our way in the BRICs. We are currently looking at things in India and China, but I intend to complete with the other two and set foot in Africa. If you buy from them, you already have half the way to sell to them.

–Of course, if footwear is your thing, it's good to put both feet everywhere.

–Hahaha! Yes, and we have come a long way! The thing is, we have three factories, two in Europe and one recently opened in China. I'm really scared of the Chinese, Leo. With what we have saved in a year by closing another one we had, the investment is already back due to the labor differential. Seeing this, my directors ask like crazy that we repeat the move with one of the other two factories.

Pietro knows perfectly well that his problem is quite common nowadays, as are his doubts. China has become the factory of the world, and a lot of money is changing hands. I have seen traditional families ruined overnight by this effect in many countries, especially in the textile sector. For my part, it is still enriching to know their cases firsthand.

–You are not afraid of the Chinese. What scares you is not knowing what will happen to those tons of American currency they are pocketing, and if suddenly, one day they will end up plundering what you have invested. But please go on, tell me more.

–Right, so far, nothing that is not *vox populi*. The thing is, I work in luxury footwear, and besides, almost all our models are handmade. Our lasts are centuries old and live under the dome of a Swiss bank. Of course, what I manufacture today in China are those mass-produced models. You can also imagine that they spare no effort to copy our technology, fortunately still with poor results, but that may change one day. On the other hand, our value is the logo. You know that the Italian brand sells very well abroad, it's what we do best in this country.

–Yes, yes, yes. Almost all Spanish olive oil goes to the final consumer with your flag on the bottle, and at enriched uranium prices, that's a fact.

–Yes, as it is also a fact, the conceptual war of elegance in footwear is hundreds of years old. Our paradigm is that the foot should rest in a cloud, and the English paradigm is that the shoe should be uncomfortable, and as soon as it is shaped to the foot, it should be replaced. Aside from romanticism, this makes it much easier for the English to manufacture their top-line shoes and replace them. We manufacture to last: our shoe is a Vespa. This struggle will not cease to be exclusive to Italy and England, at least as long as there are gentlemen in the world and it is their wives who come into the store to buy their shoes and, as long as it lasts, the value of the top brand will be good support for the second brands of the house.

–Are there any strong groups that are likely to buy your company in the medium or long term?

–Well, in monetary terms, any Arab investment fund or Western pension fund, to say the least, is interested, and they have never failed to make offers that far exceed the real present or future value of the company. We have always refused them. This is tradition, almost a matter of state. When the Pope wears Prada shoes on a diplomatic visit or the President of France wears one of our models to Brussels to make a speech, it is never a coincidence. It's solemn nonsense - here, he frowns and bites his ring. I hadn't noticed it before. Could Pietro be another Italian prince?

–So, excuse my frankness, what worries you is that with the evolution of the markets, this paradigm will soon change, and the reason for having our lasts stored in a Swiss bank will be lost. They will become nothing more than mere curiosity in a museum in Shanghai, right? - I have hit the nail on the head, considering his expression.

–Exactly! Are the Chinese going to impose their ways and customs on us in the long run, or will we keep our hand on the tiller of black label products? They're getting fat on money, and their culture is five thousand years old. We managed to hold them in check with the little red book all this time, but that's over. At the rate we are going, the whole planet will be genetically and culturally unified in four generations or so, and there are many millions of them. I understand that this is a subject worthy of a business psychologist.

–I'm certainly not going to be the one to teach you how to sell shoes. It's even more geopolitics than pure business what you're proposing to me. Wow! Let me go to the restroom and order an *amaretto* and see if I can spit out a coherent first idea. Girls! I'm going to stop by the bar. Can I get you anything? - What green eyes, mother of mine…

I like the debate that Pietro raises. I will have to remember to take some notes tomorrow because whatever I tell him today will be quite basic. I'll also have to consider looking for an Asian project to see what's going on over there and buy some translated books. I still don't have time to learn Mandarin. I go back to the table with some mental sketch. My amaretto is waiting for me. As I sit down, Lucia questions me.

–Leo, I couldn't help overhearing your conversation, and I'm eager to hear your response.

She's eager! And look at me paying attention to her choice of words, and her body language, AND her body! I have to heed my emotional deontology and keep fighting for naturalness. Lucia is knocking down too many barriers, too fast. It's been a long time since I had to think about putting myself on guard. And I read in Sandra's eyes that she is laughing inside. This girl has been talking too much behind my back. Well, I'm going to be okay with my analysis.

–I am still chewing on ideas. I ask you to give me half an *amaretto,* so I don't make a fool of myself. In the meantime, you can help me. What do you think about it, Lucia?

–I'm a little lost, too. We have a lot of problems right now with the real estate slump. Dad is desperate. No one is buying his properties, and interest rates are going up all the time. If things keep going like this, I'm going to have to get involved with, I don't know, a prestigious consultant, for example - I think I'm livid.

–Hahaha! - I burst out. Laughter always breaks up any embarrassing situation, as Voltaire well knew. The other three are staring at us. I'm going to kill the Paulist. - Of course, the real estate fall highlights your good humor, Lucia. Well, tonight you will be the dance partner of one of us, although I don't know how my prestige is around here - I give Sandra a murderous look - I can speak in the voices of my most prestigious colleagues. Of course, depending on how sexy you've chosen the *bustier,*

I might also tell you about my exploits and omit the others while keeping my hand on your heart.

I just saved myself by the skin of my teeth. Lucia blushes slightly and breaks off with a giggle that is followed by the rest of us. The tension and a long drink of *amaretto* loosen my tongue on the subject of Pietro.

–Let's go there, Pietro. This is not consulting, but still an informal talk and very impromptu. First of all, we want to know what will happen with China and Europe and luxury goods in that context. As I see it, the Global Village is already a reality. Continents become zones, and countries become neighborhoods, isn't it?

–That's right, - Pietro replies, poking his nose over his cup of *cappuccio*.

–We are also detecting specific press trends: The United States as a gendarme, China: the factory, India: the software planet, Europe: services and tourism, Africa and South America: food and raw materials. It is a very generalist vision, I know. I want us to picture the world as a cake that was already caricatured in Garibaldi's time. As far as I am concerned, the matter's psychological vision and not the crystal ball, Internet and cable television are the two great cultural binders. Wa... Sandra will confirm that in the slums, access to cable TV is "free" in quotation marks. The fact is that access is favored to the lowest incomes for the sake of spreading the common language.

Sandra moves her lips silently. She is calling me "Filho da puta". I nod to her contentedly, smiling and unseen by others.

–This scenario indicates that in Asia, too, there will be homogenization. To impose their criteria and keep their factories alive, they will have to use their dollars in their territory and abroad. On the other hand, I bring here an apparently simplistic but very revealing analogy for the case at hand: the Marco Polo expedition. The great Khan receives with honors the Polo family while inaugurating the silk route, from which we learn everything from the use of paper to *fettucini*. The pope himself, however, turns a deaf ear to Kubilai's request for a hundred engineers. I don't know if Kubilai included your lasts in that message, but it certainly shows the way: trade yes, technology no. Europe is jealous of its science. In any case, the Polos are taking back the august Vatican blessing under their arms - Chloé digresses.

–Certainly, the blessing did not succeed in making Christianity spread to China. If it had, you would have a large Vatican branch in Shanghai today.

–Excellent point, Chloé. Now let's move on to socials. Our Western model is individualistic, while the Chinese model is collectivist. This affects the desire's mechanism, which is what drives people to shopping malls. Luckily for you, our model is very contagious, and Hong Kong has served as a guinea pig to prove this point. The luxury market is nothing more than the ultimate extrapolation of mass desire. Elites are opinion formers to a certain extent. There is a return effect. If the prince defines a product as desirable and does not get the people to desire it by making its consumption synonymous with social success, that product will not work. If I were to transform this talk into a serious consultancy, the first thing I would do is study the opium wars and their implications for Chinese high society. I would also dig into the history books for each dynasty's palace intrigues and draw parallels with ours and their motivations. Then I would make a statistic of the pathologies in the dragon empire and establish comparisons in behaviorism. Only then would I give you an appointment to deliver a review.

–You remind me of a diplomat: you light the way without advancing on it - Pietro comments - but it works. You make me curious.

–It's not a bad comparison. Sometimes my role is confused with that of a strategy consultant. Based on your structure and the market, the strategy consultant proposes a range of solutions and gives his recommendations. He is well rid of providing an absolute hypothesis to get out of it if his model fails. My job is not to think for you. My job is to force you to judge based on new elements. To force you to think, and then force you back again, until you are the one who finds the solution that suits you best. When I'm done with you is when the strategy comes and, if I've done it reasonably well, you're ready to receive it and get the best out of it. Then I take the pulse of what you have decided to carry out and the new doubts you will have. Don't be surprised if I tell you that, with a thorough study, you might be able to glimpse coherent reasons why it would be worth your while to get rid of your lasts.

–I doubt that very much, but I won't put my hand in the fire. Worse things have been seen. I reckon there is a certain mystique about the lasts. They motivate me.

–Look, - I tell him, taking a notebook out of the briefcase, - take a look at this and see if it inspires you. It's confidential, and it's in progress, and I can show it to you. It might put your imagination to work in new ways.

THE BLACK LABEL INSTITUTE
Consumer market stratification project.

Pietro rolls up his sleeves, puts his glasses on, and starts reading. The project I'm showing him is an amalgam of the Michelin guide, consumer magazines, and the Internet. The idea is to create a black label management entity. The black label is a compelling archetype, too often exploited by marketing departments in a very irresponsible way. Based on individual quality and opinion criteria, the institute issues a black label, the same one, for each brand on the market, regardless of what this brand has determined as a top product. The same black label for all products, for all countries and managed by an independent think tank that seeks only to promote luxury standardization. It doesn't matter if it's cars, yogurts, clothes, services, whatever. Each active catalog, each set of products or services will have a black mark attributed by the institute. The consumer will know that the producing company has had nothing to do with the attribution, except for the excellence applied in its production. Each manufacturing company is free to place the institute's label on the product concerned.

–A market study has been carried out. We have already obtained the approval of several institutions in Brussels and Washington and an investment bank whose name I don't want to remember. - While Pietro is reading, the rest of us start to organize the meeting. It is almost seven o'clock.

–This is a bomb, Leo! Can I have a copy? I'd like to dedicate a weekend to it.

–I can't, Pietro. But if you give it some thought and are interested in the subject, you can participate in the pilot, we'll see how. This project was originally a free and global trademark registry: ideas looking for funding and money looking for ideas with its royalty mechanism, without the intervention of the traditional bodies, and interlinked with the UN. We didn't like the concept and took advantage of the development team. See you tonight. Shall we go, Sandra? A kiss to all. Chloé, I hope you come and pick us up tomorrow if we end up at the police station. I've seen many watts of sound coming out of those trucks in front of the Duomo.

–Don't worry, Leo. I'll have some aspirin canteens ready just in case. Have a good time. Kiss.

5 Wandra

The sea was like a plate full of oil. The summer sun formed a fantastic mosaic of light points on the water, and some merchant ships came and went meekly in front of the *Beira-Mar* avenue in Florianópolis. Wanderleia walked on her plastic flip-flops among the few idlers who, not yet having decided on their Sunday activities, strolled aimlessly along the cobblestone sidewalk.

It was midday. In those latitudes, the sun's rays fall perpendicularly, drenching the skulls with torrid languor. It isn't very easy to think of anything concrete in such a situation. She did not realize it, but her swagger diverted the eyes of some passers-by. Nor had it bothered her since she was a child. The wiggle was utterly natural, a product of her racial mix and that old mystery whereby all her compatriots were born with their spines uncrossed and curved forward. The price to pay for the uplifted arse was the no less famous and sensual belly.

She had a date with some friends. They were all going to a churrasco at Celia and João's house. The night before, she had had to take a group of European ecologists staying at the hotel she was managing to a *candomblé terreiro,* and it had gone on until the wee hours. She hesitated between having the first chopp of the day to get rid of the headache or a fruit juice. Her favorite was *acerola* with orange. She always defended the goodness of chopp, which was more like a cereal juice, a little overdone but very healthy since it was not pasteurized. By a festive association of ideas, she finally decided on *açaí* from the cart of an athletic mulatto who announced the product loudly to the rhythm of an imaginary samba.

Açaíí for me, açaí for you! Buy my açaiíí!
Açaiíí!

Açaí is an Amazonian berry with mysterious priapic and regenerative virtues. It does not travel well, so it only comes out of the Amazon frozen and the juice houses, real laboratories, combine it with natural guarana, proteinate or whatever, in formulas worthy of the Wild West peddlers. In contrast to the latter, *açaí* does its job exceptionally well.

It had only been three years since she had changed her name, and she was still getting used to it. She did it not so much for her ex-husband, whose mother could not stand the idea of her daughter-in-law being so Brazilian. She had always nurtured her little son's dream of marrying a gringa and had taken every opportunity to send the boy to study abroad. She had her name changed as a ritual of renewal. Her childhood had been miserable.

Wanderleia lost her virginity at the age of twelve at a funk dance. She was not one of the first of her generation, far from it, but the circumstances were unexpectedly sordid. The neighborhood dealer, whom she already knew because her older brother made ends meet by selling a few bags, seduced her on the dance floor and took her to a secluded spot where they began their trysts. She let herself go, and the heartless man began to throw perfume in her face. No sooner had she regained her spatial awareness than she found that the man who was finishing off her enjoyment was not the one who had taken her to that corner. Even worse, he was wearing a military police uniform, and she could see behind him another uniformed man who was putting his pants back on.

She wished with all her heart that she could rip the sweaty macaque's member off, but she knew it would get worse, and evil was already done anyway. She stood trembling in the corner until her friends found her there, in a fetal position, her favorite skirt stained with blood, aching and sobbing. She did not want to report it. She had heard terrible stories from the few who had dared to do so, and, with law enforcement officers involved in the case, she knew it would do little good. Her greatest fear was that her father would find out and the pregnancy, which, fortunately, did not occur.

What had happened to Wanderleia was and still is commonplace, not only in Brazil and in humble environments. It left her upset to the point of attempting suicide. She was placed in a shelter, where her companions treated her even worse than the favela. This, instead of making her sink, turned her into a strong and determined woman and, a few years later, she managed to enjoy sex for the first time. No longer as a bargaining chip but as a true expression of tenderness and love.

She helped her mother sell fruit in the market, and her mother, in turn, tirelessly explained to her that the only way out of there for her was to study, study without stopping work, and marry an honest man, as wealthy as possible. She had seven brothers and sisters on her mother's side and another thirteen on her father's side. She was the second to last. In her unpainted brick cottage, eleven souls slept in the same room. There were only three old books for all the children, but only she and her sister Jaquelaine paid attention to them. It was only through the constant rereading of these three books that she discovered her passion for literature. A dilapidated *História Ilustrada do Brasil*, a comic book of *Mônica,* and a Bible in even worse condition. She always carried with her an image of San Expedito to escape that wheel of misery. It was her grandmother, the Bahian, who taught her devotion to the saint of urgent causes. She called him *São Xixí* because of the physiological urgency.

They arrived at the churrasco first. João was preparing the fire for the grill, and the oven he had in the backyard, and Celia was putting the finishing touches on her new recipe for cod with hearts of palm. Celia loved to improvise cod recipes. She always said that it was her duty to help get to four hundred if there are three hundred official recipes. They were both middle-aged and had met years ago in São Paulo at a Tim Maia concert. João was bald and had worked in a steel mill as a child. One drunken day he told them that you had to give head in the blast furnaces to get a cigarette. He had picked up the smoking habit much younger. After six months of metalworking, he decided not to go back to kneeling, smoked his last cigarette, and since then could not stand the smell of tobacco. Today they both ran a bar downtown, had two grown children, and promised each other a sweet golden age.

People were arriving. Among the guests were five musicians. In Celia and João's house, it was almost sacred to end the Sunday churrasco with live music and dancing, and this was not going to be an exception. Equally sacred was to bring a bottle or specialty. Wanderleia had brought a bottle of *Terra Vermelha*, an organic *cachaça*, a gift from the gringos the night before. João officiated as bbq master, and it was all delicious. While they ate and chatted animatedly, some watched soccer on TV, and the kids were swimming in the pool. The radio was trying to make itself heard without any success.

–Sandra, you are about to celebrate two years of work at the hotel. How are you doing?

–I love it, I'm learning a lot, and I'm meeting a lot of people. The gringos are even weirder than I thought. They all arrive with somber faces and make a drama out of everything. Whether they come for work or pleasure, it's as if they landed from another planet.

–I suppose you make an effort to change their attitude. We have to promote tourism. Are you still determined to live in the hotel? My uncle is renting some spectacular apartments, with security and everything. Hey Manuel, that's my beer!

–It doesn't matter who it's from. If you don't drink it, it gets hot. Open another one! And my name is not Manuel.

–I'm staying at the hotel. It is very nice and, with the savings, I want to pay for a holiday in New York. I have never left Mercosur.

–What a shame, you were going to love the apartments. Hey, do many Argentines go there? At the current exchange rate, the "brothers" must be coming like flies to honey. Hey, Manuel! I just opened that beer. It's mine. The other Manuel has already stolen the last one!

–Excuse me, girl, what a temper… I'll take one, do you have a callus on your foot?

–Is everyone's name Manuel here?

–I don't know anyone today. For me, they are all Manuel. Well, if I get happy, they are all *gorgeous*. I don't let go of the can anymore. Were you telling me about the Argentines?

–Yes, more of them are coming. The wind will change, as always. My last boyfriend was from Clorinda. It was beautiful while it lasted.

–You should start thinking about getting married. Don't you want to have children?

–Ufa! Not yet. My mother also says the same thing every time we talk. I want to give myself time to travel. I've already been married. All this year, I have been visiting with the agency many things I didn't know: the waterfalls on both sides, the Jesuit ruins in Paraguay, Montevideo. I don't know. I miss a little love, but freedom has its nice parts. I want to go to Europe too, alone and without commitment.

–A chicken heart? A sausage? A French kiss?

–Bring here some sausages and keep dreaming! When you have a job, maybe we'll clean up your drool, Manuel. You're very lacking. Can you count? Then don't count on me!

–Cruel and ruthless woman, when you see me dance, you will regret it… I am a slave to love! It's part of my show!

–And I'm a saintly sinner! Come on, if you hook *picanha*, come back here! He's funny, isn't he?

–He's funny, yes. But for me today, I'm neither short nor tall. I'm exhausted from yesterday. You're not very close to getting married either, are you?

–I raise my daughter alone and wouldn't bring a man into the house for all the gold in the world. The girl's father was an evangelical and a drunkard, alternately. Every month he did one thing, carefully following the calendar. Either in the bar or the temple. He was a hard worker, yes, but you can't imagine the war he gave me. I remain a teacher, mother, and single. Let men give me eternal love for no more than a week. Then they spoil everything.

–My father was a drunkard too. He always said that his religion was limited to being a son of God and that everything else was extra. Now he doesn't drink anymore. He's a good man, he's been selling matte on the sidewalk all his life, and he has always respected my mother. Now he has lost all his teeth and does not want me to buy him a set of teeth because he says that a macho man who is a macho man takes what he gets.

–Hahaha, how cute! When you come to my place, I'll throw you the *búzios*. Let's see what the *orixás* have to say about your traveling projects. Have another beer!

–Your *picanha*, ladies, courtesy of the most gallant man of the party.

–What a delight! Thank you, "slave to love" Where are you from, Manuel?

–I am Luiz, a carioca in red. Good at dancing and better in bed. They are starting with the samba wheel. Do you dance, princess?

–I dance! But don't get your hopes up, shorty. Are you coming, Sandra?

–I'm going to check out that flambéed banana that's going around first. I'll see you later.

–Ask the monkey if he likes bananas…

Music was warming up the atmosphere. Few resisted the call of the *surdo*, the lowest drum, apparently the easiest to play. It is not. It sets the baseline for the rest. Without good *surdo,* there is no good samba. Similar scenes were taking place all over the country at that time. It is challenging to be Brazilian and go twelve months in a row without a good Sunday churrasco. Wanderleia held out until sunset. She conveniently said goodbye to the hosts and boarded the bus that would drop her off at the hotel's door. She had experienced several muggings on the bus, but that did not frighten her at all. Instead, it inflamed her. Her war was to fight for the way things should be. She thought that if good people were intimidated by crime, evil would have won the battle, which seemed unacceptable. She'd better put her own life at risk than giving way to resignation.

She was also convinced that those who had suffered nothing in their lives had not reached maturity. In the favela, one learns to dance with precariousness. At her age, she was already discovering that, from that daily precariousness, her people obtained the unsuspected reward of much more intense moments of happiness when things went well. Making long-term plans was a complete folly for her. As Zeca sings, "I let life take me." As Martinho sings, "Life is going to get better." Few peoples have a musical tradition so impervious to outside influence. Samba is a sonorous instruction manual shared by all and slowly evolving. If the lyrics of a song endure, and they can endure for a very long time, it is the result of a natural popular referendum. Similar to the song of the Yubarta whales. A whole existential school and a strong social glue.

She arrived at the hotel with her legs numb with fatigue. Her whole body was screaming for a hot bath. She stopped at the front desk to see if there were any messages for her. At this, she passed a European couple who were complaining to the receptionist.

–Miss, I demand to speak with management. We had reserved the presidential suite. You can't tell us it's been already taken!

–But sir, in any case, the error is of the agency with which you have contracted the trip. I just showed you the reservation form that was sent to us. It's Sunday, and the manager has the day off - they had instructions not to identify her to anyone not on duty and complied carefully, but the poor receptionist was having a hard time.

–Look, either you give me a decent solution, or I don't know what I'm going to do, but it's not going to be good. My girlfriend is about to faint! The flight has been hellish, and it is not tolerable that you want to put me in a standard room.

Wanderleia went to the restroom and called the front desk on her cell phone.

–Joana, hold the downpour a little longer, tell the gentleman that you will reach me on my phone, and pass it on to me.

She waited five minutes and answered the call. After Joana's explanation, the client came on and didn't let her speak for a long time with his argument.

–Gentleman, I beg your pardon. I understand that Joana is not at fault, and the presidential room is taken. Nevertheless, we offer you the bridal room prepared for a couple that should arrive later. It has silk sheets, chocolates, flowers, and French champagne at a convenient temperature. The view is better than the presidential room and, for compensation, I offer you a free dinner in our restaurant tomorrow night, if you wish. What do you think?

–Thank God, at last something reasonable! I'm happy to accept. Sorry for the inconvenience on a Sunday. I'll put you through to the receptionist.

–Joana, listen carefully. You tell them that, while the suite cools down, which must be sweltering, I insisted on inviting them to a *caipirinha* at the piano bar. You take charge of their luggage and send two bellboys and four maids to transform my apartment into a bridal suite, to make everything spotless in record time, and to take my things from the bathroom and closet to 512, which is free. The rest of my belongings shall go to the storage room. You give me the keys to 512 without a peep. It is essential to leave welcome cards with the names of another couple on the bedside tables.

–Yes, ma'am, we will. Good Sunday, and excuse the call.

She hung up just in time. On her way out, the European woman was entering the toilet. She picked up the key as planned. The man was visibly relieved and what to say about Joana! She locked herself in the room to wait for her belongings and, when they arrived, without ordering anything, she threw herself on the bed and fell into a deep sleep.

The next day went by as usual. Wanderleia had chosen a pink *tailleur* halfway between nondescript and chic, according to her criteria. She wore her abundant hair in a Japanese bun crossed with a silver chopstick brought by a friend of hers who owned a sushi bar in São Paulo. In the late afternoon, she wanted to talk to the photographer who was doing a garden session. The man, a tall, gangly white man, had been photographing the same pineapple for seven hours. He moved a lot and fluidly. His square glasses covered most of his face.

–Hi Francis, when I gave you permission for the session, I thought this would be full of swimsuit models, and I was a little excited. But I've been watching you all day, and my jaw is on the floor. Seven technicians and a photographer for a pineapple seem a bit much.

–Hello, sea goddess, hahaha! The pineapple is an ad for the tourism department. I chose your garden because of the sea's angle with the island in the background, and the light seemed appealing to me. I am thrilled. It has been a spectacular day. I have almost two thousand shots.

–Two thousand photos of the same pineapple?

–Yes, goddess, I work with nuance. People think magic is just snapping their fingers. There is a lot of magic in this. There's light, there's air, there's temperature, there's my mood. Do you think the pineapple is still? For me, it's been dancing all day. Marcelo! That flower is no good to me anymore! Call Adriana and have her send another one, a little bigger this time!

–I'm curious. Why doesn't the flower work for you? I see it perfectly - Wanderleia pinched her nose.

–It is magic, goddess, magic. That flower is a hibiscus. Hibiscus of that size is only found in Búzios. Adriana called me last month to tell me that she had located a bush a few blocks from here. Now she is on duty in front of the bush and is sending me the flowers. They only last half an hour out of the ground, Marcelo! 30 degrees to the right, focus three! And increase the power!

—And wouldn't it have been easier to do the session in Búzios?

—Oh goddess, everything must be explained to you. It is very rare, I told you. It is the combination. In Búzios, I don't see the light of Florianópolis. In Búzios, I see the light of Búzios. Whoever sees the photo will see, like you, one more pineapple, without knowing that it is the most special pineapple he has ever seen in his life. That's the magic, don't look for three feet to the cat. That pineapple has to have more strength in its conception than a fashion show. That pineapple is going to represent the country in a lot of audiovisual material. I'm not going to send it off by taking three pictures of it in the market!

—Spectacular, as you say... Are you missing something? A magic pineapple juice?

—You can make jokes. I'm used to it. I'm not going to tell you about the editing sessions the final photo will undergo in the studio. Remember this. If I take a high-quality recorder and stick my tongue in your ear while recording your sigh, I capture a piece of you. Suppose tomorrow you become famous for whatever, and I ask a DJ friend to include in a mix a complete treatment of the sigh without telling him where it comes from. In that case, the chances are that, out of the whole album that DJ releases, the most outstanding track will be the one with the sigh. And I won't tell you more, because then everything is public. I don't care if you believe it or not. I know it and use it. Marcelo! Thirty degrees, I said! Are you deaf?

Wanderleia returned a snowy smile. She belonged to the indeterminate group known in Brazil as criollos. The common denominator of those too light to be mulatto and too dark to be white. Her perfect teeth betrayed the African presence in her veins despite her lank toupee hair and fairly fair skin. He headed for the bar to send Francis a pineapple juice made with her own hands. She crushed some fresh mint leaves on top of the juice. There was something powerful about that idea of magic.

She finished dinner in the hotel kitchen. The chef had saved her a portion of his reinterpretation of the classic *feijoada*, which he knew she loved. Just beans, boneless duck confit, and sun-dried meat with a few slices of orange. She headed to the dining room to introduce herself to the Europeans who had evicted her the night before.

–Good evening. I am Sandra Gomes, the hotel manager. We spoke on the phone yesterday. Did you like the room?

They were having dessert. She had a stracciatella ice cream, and he had a flambéed mango crêpe. The man stood up to greet her, wiping his thin beard with his napkin. His girlfriend had eyes as green as the sea. He was surprised he hadn't noticed them last night.

–As you may know from last night's little incident, my name is Pietro Scandia. We are tremendously grateful for your kindness. This is my partner. Lucia.

–My pleasure. Hey, weren't you at the reception yesterday?

–You must have crossed paths with my sister, who has come to visit me and is staying at the hotel - her confidence disarmed Lucia - Hahaha! We look alike, don't we? We've always been told so. Was the dinner to your liking? - she was relieved to see that they had been kind enough to order a national wine. Sometimes those invitations could turn into nonsense.

–Everything was perfect, - he answered. - I especially liked the *cavaquinha*. I didn't know that lobster cousin.

–I have been worried about the newlyweds who have lost their rooms. What happened to them?

–Don't worry about them. They have also had an upgrade in the bridal suite at another hotel chain, very close to here. I saw them this morning, and they were beaming.

–Give me your card, please. And your foot number. I am a shoe manufacturer and would like to reciprocate.

–Here is my card. Don't worry about the shoes. It's enough for me to know that you are comfortable. If you want to gratify us anyway, give Joana a treat. She is an exceptional girl. How long are you staying in Brazil?

–Just three more days. We have been to Minas and Rio and are going down to Buenos Aires. We will return to Italy from there. Here is my card. Be sure to call us if one day you are the one crossing the pond.

–I will be happy to do so, thank you very much. Enjoy your stay with us. And sorry for any inconvenience.

Lucia did not seem to be amused by the way Pietro was looking at Sandra. A few seconds too long. Sandra politely vanished with the satisfaction of duty well done.

6 Via fatebenefratelli

–What does Fatebenefratelli mean, Leo? It sounds like the name of a pasta restaurant. It's hilarious.

–"Do good, brothers," or something like that. It refers to the Little Brothers of St. John. A hospital order that has a lot of hospitals.

We both walk to the apartment. I'm carrying my tuxedo, freshly dyed, and Sandra is hanging on my other arm. We look like a couple in love on vacation in Milan. I like to feel like the protagonist of a Doisneau scene. When I feel like this, time goes slower. We get into the elevator, one of those old-fashioned wooden glass elevators that you have to open by hand. As we enter the floor, she hands me one of the bags she was carrying.

–Take this, honey. I bought you a present to show you I was delighted with your invitation to this trip. Besides, I think there's going to be something with Pietro. We are both free, and there is chemistry going on. It's nicer than when I met them in Brazil.

–Thank you very much, bitch. You always know how to make yourself forgive in advance. I don't want to know what you said to Lucia while I was in the gallery's bathroom. Let's see...

I open the package and find, to my enormous satisfaction, a sea urchin opening scissors. I love it! It is a very difficult gadget to find, especially outside of France. When you find it, you can also be disappointed that the quality is deplorable and breaks after the first dozen. This one looks perfect.

–It's fantastic, Sandra! You couldn't have picked a better gift. I'll have to check my luggage so that the airport won't steal it from me. Where did you find this wonder?

–I saw it in the window of an antique cutlery shop. A real Ali-Baba's cave. They only sell knives, and they have everything. Tomorrow, if you want, we shall go back. I remembered when the four of us went to Ubatuba together when we were still married to our exes. That day, with the sea urchins, your hands were all scratched because of the sewing scissors.

–I love it. I love it! Thank you so much. Hug me, come on. Dinner's on me today.

We each go into our rooms to use those patrician bathtubs for the first time. I get rid of the suit and go with the laptop to turn on the water. The spray is impressive. It's nice. The last bathtub I had, took almost three-quarters of an hour to fill because of the rickety pressure. In winter, it wasn't easy to keep the water temperature. I put a record of Vinicius de Moraes, immortal bard, in the living room, in honor of my guest. After all, she made my day with her gift. *Para viver um grande amor* is playing. I dive under the foam and start checking my emails. Marco has made the transfer, meaning the invoice was authorized yesterday, and his subtle mafia threat this morning was a joke. Nice guy, this Marco.

To live a great love, you need a lot of concentration and a lot of wisdom.
A lot of seriousness and little laughter, to live a great love.
To live a great love, it is necessary to be a one-woman man.
Because to belong to many, of course, is for those who want to, and has no value.
To live a great love, one must first become a gentleman

And to be his lady's entirely, however that may be.
One must make the body a dwelling where the beloved
woman can cloister herself
And to behave from the outside with a sword, to live a
great love.

A lot of seriousness to live a great love, poet, a lot of seriousness. The bath is giving me a mud massage. Olympus must have baths like this. I lose track of time, wrapped in my ramblings and remembering Lucia's eyes. Suddenly, Sandra appears wrapped in a towel and with her hair tied up.

–Love, my bathtub has no water. I come to bathe here.

Without giving me time to answer, she drops her towel to the floor, revealing her sculpted body. She is completely depilated, and there are traces of the slight bikini marks that are iconic in her homeland.

–Do you want to kill me? Hey, I'm a rock, but I'm not made of stone!

–You've already seen me naked several times on the nude beach, - she protests as she gently climbs into the bathtub. - If you like what you see, so much the better. There, you get hot before the party and explore your possibilities with Lucia. We agreed that, as long as nothing happens between the two of us, we are almost brothers, right? Stop complaining and tell me where we are having dinner.

–Well, girl. The beach was the beach, not a Roman bath. And, in the Bible, the incest thing is very relative. Look at the case of Lot's daughters! I'll think I'm Ulysses stuck with a mermaid in the bathtub, with my hands tied and no wax in my ears -I sigh for a long time-. I'm still with polenta in my throat. I prefer something light. It's not the ideal place, but how about some sushi?

–Sushi sounds great to me! Look for a good one on the Internet.

–There it is! I found it, and it's not far away. I'm going to shave now. Enjoy your bath, mermaid -I get out of the tub, awkwardly trying to hide my embarrassment-. And let's drop Portuguese and switch to Spanish. My poor Italian is suffering more than it should.

-*Vaaale.* Hey, Ulysses, you seem to like what you see. Don't thank me.

–*Hija de puta...*

I must say that I like waxed women quite a bit. A girlfriend I had in Barcelona insisted that I wax my whole body. It is widespread nowadays, but for many things I stick to the twentieth century and for many others to the nineteenth. Very serious, poet.

As Sandra finishes bathing, I can't help but go to her bathroom to check if she lied to me about water in her bathtub. She hasn't lied to me. I call to book a table. I had already heard good things about the restaurant, but I still don't know it. I love the name: *General Company of Travelers, Navigators, and Dreamers.* A toast to Ulysses. I intend to arrive at the party around eleven o'clock, so we are on schedule. It doesn't look like it's going to rain today, nor is it too cold. I inform my mermaid that we will dress up after dinner.

We get out of the cab in front of the restaurant. It is advertised as a Japanese *trattoria* and, upon entering, we see that the description lives up to the place. Warm, cozy, and with classic *trattoria* furniture. If it were not for the decoration and unmistakable rice vinegar smell, one would think that the cuisine is regional. We are received very kindly. I always associate good sushi with the tatami, but I have also had pleasant surprises without it and some unpleasant ones eating in the lotus position. The maître comes to take our order, and Sandra takes the helm.

–Is your sushi man Japanese? If so, I would like to meet him.

–Yes, he's new, and we're testing him. It looks good. I wasn't going to tell you anything else, either. Just a moment, I'll see if he can come by. Drinks?

–Chilled sake for two, is that okay with you, Leo?

–It sounds great to me - it's the first time I've let myself get carried away in a restaurant outside of Brazil by Sandra.

A short, stocky Japanese man with a spotless uniform and three knives around his waist approaches us. I have a lot of respect for sushi knives, which cut like real katanas, since one day I left a piece of skin from my index finger on the cutting board with one of them. If the Japanese guy carrying them doesn't smile, I'm on my guard too. This one smiles.

–*Konnichi wa.*

–*Konnichi wa.*

–*Watashi wa Gomes Sandra desu. Hajimemashite.* - My eyebrows go up on the back of my head. I can't believe she´s speaking Japanese! I had no idea. The two engage in a lively conversation that I don't even hear the cook's nods. When they seem to have finished, I whisper to Sandra.

–What did you ask him?

–Oh, I'm sorry, I haven't asked him for anything yet, - she says, pointing at the table with her index finger in circles, - *Omakase!*

–*Hai. Hai.* - he answers, smiling.

–*Arigato, Suzuki san*, - she says as the man walks back to the kitchen.

–That dish has to be plentiful. Do you only order one thing? I'm hungry!

–No, you fool! Haha! *Omakase* means I let him decide. Take it as if it were a surprise menu, but never order it yourself if the cook doesn't like you. That is if you don't want to leave your shirt or your guts.

Mr. Suzuki has undoubtedly taken a liking to Sandra. Our neighbors at the table look at us enviously throughout the meal. Just from the colorfulness and presentation, coupled with my murmurs of delight at every bite, it's clear we've received favored treatment. Suzuki san has just given us a master class in fusion. If you had told me that you could marry fresh grilled foie with sundried tomato and oyster with jelly, my hair would have stood on end. How I will miss this girl when she returns to Oviedo and I have to go eat Japanese!

–Hey Sandra, when we go out, put in a good word for me with this Japanese magician. I can't live without repeating something like that! Where did you learn Japanese?

–As a child, I helped my mother in the market for years, and the family in the stall next door was Japanese. There are many in São Paulo. They have always been very welcome because they can plant tons in ridiculous spaces. There was a boy my age who taught me everything I know. Back then, it was like a game. I don't think I would be able to learn it today. It has been very good for me professionally. Japanese clients are very grateful. They are not used to being received in their language. When you come to see me, I'll take you to a place I know that makes a red baby octopus to die for.

–That is if you don't end up staying in Europe. I'm afraid your sabbatical may turn into something else. Well, who are we criticizing today?

–You're evil, Spaniard. As the Portuguese say: from Spain comes neither good wind nor good marriage - she sticks her tongue out at me.

–They say that because we don't know each other very well, only for the wrong things. We are two peoples who have lived with our backs to each other all the time. Anyway, it seems that this point is changing. I have a very fierce Basque friend who says that Portugal is the only independent region of Spain. The Basques are always at each other's throats. Have you ever been to Portugal? I think that if one day we liquidate centralism in our country, " Iberian States" with the Lusos would be viable.

–Never been. I'm looking forward to it. I know many Portuguese there. I have never been to Madrid either, except for quick trips to the airport. The first time I landed at your airport, I had the impression I was arriving on Mars. What a dry place! My lungs dried up as soon as I got out of the plane. And that futuristic monster, there, in the middle of that brown landscape. I was looking out the window, and I was a little scared.

–Madrid is quite particular. Legend has it that Castilla used to be populated by forests and that we took them all out to build ships for America's conquest. I don't know how true that is. Anyway, when you come back, you can stay at home for a few days, and I'll show it to you, see what you think. I'm not going to pass up the opportunity to get plugged by the cook at the *Ginza*.

–I'm going to miss my Spanish classes if I do that. If you promise to speak to me in Spanish all the time and correct my mistakes, I'll accept.

–If you promise me that you won't get back in my bathtub with me in it, that's a given. The size of the bathtub at home and my current celibacy would not let me endure it anymore.

–I'll do my best! How little endurance you have... Let's see if you get a girlfriend soon. You're unbearable.

–Take it as a compliment. After all, the day you don't attract men as you do now, you're going to be in for a disappointment.

–A disappointment, or a relief. I'm not quite sure. Another sake, yes, - she says, draining her wooden cup in one gulp. I find your appreciation of centralism amusing. We have capitals for everything. Even Brasilia replaced Rio de Janeiro. Every time a Carioca comes to me with a comment about his wonderful city and picks on my beloved *Sanpa*, I turn up my nose and say: "Sorry little one, in the newspapers of the metropolis, the seaside resort is not on the front page". But your regionalisms take the cake. We love each other.

–We love each other too. We just show our affection by slapping each other, and you know what they say about sleight of hand. The ones around here are not far behind, you know? They have some of the most gruesome north vs. south stories. And they never remember the Spanish domination. They forget so much about our presence that they claim the invention of the potato omelet and the trumps deck.

–Ah, trumps. What a fun game. I sure learned that fast in Oviedo. I don't know if anyone works there in the afternoons. The bars fill up with people at coffee time. What a healthy vice! It's a bit like our *bicho* game. I love popular stuff. In the end, I'm very popular! She gets into a movie star pose, we both laugh - haha!

–And how do you get on with cider? I've had some really fun cider nights.

–Well, until I discovered that I had to go to the bathroom all the time, I used to get horrified. We have chopp, which is also natural and follows the same urinary cycle. Now I like it a lot. But I miss chopp.

We spend the rest of the dinner talking about the different regions of the "bull skin". With

Sandra, I manage to lose some of the misgivings I've always had about European women. She makes me feel comfortable around her, and she is so affectionate! It took me a while at first to get used to her invasive kinesthesia, but now I would find it strange if it were otherwise. My compatriots have more of a tendency to the thistle's kinesthesia, although they have other virtues, and none of us have any choice but to adapt to the environment we live in. Then, Sandra has her fearsome tropical explosions. I think I could fall in love with her, although I would have to shake off certain continental taboos for that to be feasible. I don't manage to glimpse if she could fall in love with a guy like me, which is part of her charm.

A cousin of mine lived a few years in Salvador de Bahia and came back with the following axiom: "Look, Leonardo, the Spanish woman fucks with you in installments and in a planned way. The Brazilian one fucks with you right away and totally, but man, what a trip!"

Between laughter and provocations, we got into the cab back to the apartment to get dressed up. I can't wait to see Jéjé. He must be having a hell of a time...

7 Viale bligni

Chloé is putting on her pajamas. She has been back from the Brera art gallery talking to me about Leonardo. The truth is that the Madrilenian has his charm, although he is a little crazy. The Chinese still made sense, but by the time he got to the opium war, I was starting to feel like yawning. Pietro seemed interested, though, especially with that notebook he's been reading. And Pietro is one of the most adept at changing the subject without you knowing it if he doesn't like something. I know that! Seven years together, and I thought we had a future… It's a good thing we left and now get along well. Long live the seven-year crisis!

I'm not ready to go to a party tonight, but what a charming dress I bought! That's what I'm looking forward to. If I hadn't committed to making dinner for both of us, I would have been trying it on and on again. I don't have to do a single alteration, I can wear it today without any problems.

Luckily, the little frog is a queen at doing hairstyles. A black tie party, the "everything" Milan, and me with these hairs... What about my nails? All weapons must be sharpened. Making me go with a shrink… Boring! If he gets too involved, I'll hook up with Pietro and ruin the Brazilian's plan. I already knew that the Duke was more than grateful when he offered the shoes to the brunette in Brazil. This Pietro certainly uses his factory like other people buy drinks. His mother must be happy, that witch. Had we ever gotten married, I would have quickly applied Borgia syrup to her before she applies it to me.

It is funny how alive the notebook of grievances prevails, no matter how much time goes by, but everyone does it. Pietro was still reminding me today in the store about the time I had him waiting for an hour in New York, and in the end, I didn't take anything with me. If you go with me, you don't complain afterward. If you don't, you don't go with me, and I'm equally happy. They think they're doing us a favor. Then they drool if you've got the right outfit, and they destroy you if they see a wrinkle.

I've been rummaging through the pantry for a while now, and I can't think of anything. How weird is Chloé! How can anyone say they don't like pasta? I think they do it to show off. It's like saying you don't like bread or water. Look, a can of curry. I take some breasts out of the freezer, a red onion, put some rice, and that's it. If the nun doesn't learn to cook, she's going to die of disgust. Let's see what she's going to give her children if she has them one day. She says she's looking forward to it. Do I have pita bread? Yes, that's perfect. I've already settled dinner. Some endive with gorgonzola for starters, and as a dessert, there's ice cream. I don't know whether to put the walnuts in the endives or the curry. I'll put a little bit in each. I'm going to put a prosecco in to cool and take a shower.

–Hey, Joan of Arc! I told you not to smoke joints in the apartment. You'll kill my *feng shui*! Use the terrace, come on!

–With the cold weather? You're nuts! You'll get your *feng shui* back when I'm gone. It's not like I come to see you every month! Besides, when you came to Lyon, you broke my feng shui with Antoine and brought it home right under my nose. Have you seen me complaining until today? No, uh? Here, go on, puff, and give yourself a break. It seems to me that you have become jealous of that Sandra, am I wrong?

–I haven't touched one of those since my master's degree, but come on! There's a party today, and I'm not sure if I'm in the mood for it. Me, jealous? What are you talking about? I have nothing to defend.

–If you say so… I don't talk much, but I look a lot, and without your owl eyes, I see things just the same.

–Don't mess with my eyes. You know very well that they have always given me a complex! I'm not smoking anymore. There won't be enough eye drops to hide this. I'm going to take a shower. Will you comb my hair afterward?

–Yes, woman. You know it relaxes me a lot. Put on some music before you take your shower, please. Nothing too commercial. Have mercy.

–Look at the hipster! You'll have something to say about my musical tastes! I'll play whatever I want. I'm the boss in my house, and if I want to, I'll even break a plate.

I turn on the iPod, and *Je t'aime, moi non plus* starts to play. The little frog is going to think I did it on purpose. I love *random*. I'm going to pick out a tracksuit for dinner. The bathroom is warm. Living alone is great, but some things only work for two. I'm half stunned with the joint, but I couldn't remember how good it feels to take a hot shower after a few puffs.

Arghhhhh! Now I remember why I don't like reefer. I got my period in advance! The Trevi *Fountain* is already here! I'm usually like a Swiss watch. I was due the day after tomorrow! Well, dear shrink. Double challenge, Spaniard. Word of honor that today you're counting on your right hand.

I come out of the bathroom, and Paolo Conte is playing. Chloé is lying on the couch with the freezer ice mask on her face and making smoke circles with a cigarette in her *art deco* mouthpiece.

–So, will you comb my hair, Jeanne? The nickname fits you like a glove. Not because of the saint thing. You don't stop fuming! Fuck my *feng shui*…

–What a pain in the ass with the *shui-shui!* Is there *feng shui* in the tents? Come on. I'm going to make you look like a catwalk model.

–I'm going to wear my mom's wedding necklace. She beat me to it, and I got emotional.

–You'd better put on the dog's collar then. That way, anyone who comes near you will know he's looking for ruin. Look, something like that?

As if speaking French, Rufus lifts both ears and looks up at us curled up from his little bed in the corner of the living room. He is a French bulldog as good as a puppy. At the store where I bought him, all puppyish, he was the one who chose me. My language must sound right to him.

Chloé does hair like angels. In less than half an hour, she leaves me looking like I just came out of the beauty salon. I start making dinner and, while I'm blanching the onion, I let out four tears. I don't know if it's the joint or that I'm glad to have the little frog visiting me home. It was so much fun, back at the masters! It must be both. The onion is not. I never cry with onions. Pietro never understood that we women cry more when we are happy than when we are sad. At least, that's how I am. He always felt guilty. Let's see how the curry is. It's divine.

–To table, Chloé! Change the song before you sit down. Play the one you want and bring the remote control. This looks good.

I have mixed feelings about the shrink. Chloé tells me about her conversation in the cathedral. She loved it. She says he's cozy and enveloping. French women don't think like the others, anyway. As soon as they see a guy who smells like a book, they melt. I like them too. Pietro is a library on legs, but there's something uncomfortable about this one. I don't know, it's like feeling watched inside, and I don't know if I like it. The ones that see you superficially stay in the shell and are easier to carry. I think that's why I like to take care of my looks so much, so they don't go beyond the shell.

Culture is all very well, but I don't think it's the most important thing for people. What good are titles and so on if they have no sensitivity? In the end, they are conquered by sight, and we are seduced by hearing. I prefer three words of love at the right moment than *The Divine Comedy* in hendecasyllables. I am also attracted to generosity. It is easy to give everything when there is love. What is difficult is to give when there is none or when there is nowhere to scratch. I'm not going to give it importance. In the end, we barely exchanged four words. Anyway, the Brazilian said that she had noticed me smooth her way with my ex. The old trick.

–Hey, Jeanne. Do you really not want to come to the party? We were both invited. Cheer up, come on. I have a dress that would look great on you. It's almost like a cassock.

–Very funny... I won't give you any more dope if you're going to stab me like that. Look at me. Look how my pajamas have stuck to my skin. Look! And it's the bunny pajamas. Today I'm making love to Bugs Bunny.

–No more reefer. It makes me dizzy. I don't know how you can stand it. You're the smoking nun. Come on. Come on. Without you, I'll be bored out of my mind. I'll leave you a slutty dress!

–No, I'm not! I'm dying of sleep, and it will do you a lot of good if you make new friends, even if you come back empty-handed. I think you're getting used to loneliness, and I don't like to see you like this. You were always an incurable romantic. Being alone is bad for you. It darkens you. Some people are made to think, and others are made to dream. You were born to do things non-stop. Go to the party, get drunk, dance, and socialize. You'll make me happy. And I love your new dress. You're gonna break. I'll take Bugs, I'll take Rufus, I'll take my joints and your neighborhood supermarket music. A real orgy.

—You're a brat, but I love you. Kiss me. You pick this up. I have to get finished with my makeup. Make a pot of coffee for when Pietro arrives. Another little thing: my music is very good, for you to know.

As I finish the sentence, The Locomotion starts playing, back from the days when Kylie Minogue invented Katy Perry. We both stare at each other, and there is no way to hold back the laughter. This time it's not the joint. Chloé is right, I am an incorrigible romantic.

I'm lucky that Dad tolerates some breaks. He is very stern, and I think I work more with him than if I worked in a company. When I told him Chloé was coming for a week, he took it kindly, but he kept reminding me that he was marking it on his calendar with the red marker. Dad is always marking things around him with markers. If they banned them, it would make him very unhappy. He wants nothing to do with computers. He says they are the real apocalypse.

The beginning of the end of the right to privacy, he says. In a way, he's not wrong.

In Sicily, we are very attached to traditions and, even if it sounds like a cliché, almost everything that movies say is not only true but a pale shadow of reality. According to dad, my grandfather was already buying oranges just like Marlon Brando when cinema was still in black and white, and he also made olive oil.

Dad's first store was set on fire by some miscreants. According to the police, they were some guys who had had too much to drink. Dad spent the whole night on the phone, and a few days later, some men I had never seen in town came and left together in a black van.

Dad was away from home for four nights, and Mom was very worried. Then Dad showed up back, very dirty, with a huge smile and a briefcase. He fixed up his store and bought the place across the street. They never set fire to anything ever again. Two of those gentlemen came to live next door and, since then, they go everywhere with dad. He calls them "my cousins from Catania", he must think that I am not a Sicilian and that I still play with dolls.

One day a classmate of a Neapolitan friend of mine came up with the idea of writing a book. The book was later made into a documentary that became very famous. That poor boy still fears for his life. He lives in leaps and bounds, and his family is devastated. He must be in contact with the writer of Khomeini's fatwa. Maybe the two of them have gone for a drink with Bin Laden to talk about Che Guevara or Spartacus. I also know some relatives of that judge whose car was blown up, but I love my land with all my heart. I started to see the world and discovered that the same shadow lives everywhere with different surnames.

Today, you take more profit trying to fix the system from the inside than from the outside. In any case, it is of little use to overthrow it if it is then replaced by the same or worse. Evil is in our heads, and mine is blonde. It is convenient to be blonde to play stupid.

Enna is a beautiful place. It is the highest village on the island, and in winter, it is polar cold. I have a wonderful collection of sable fur hats at mom and dad's place that I only wear when I'm there. When I was a child, I thought Dr. Zhivago was a neighbor of ours, and I wanted to be like Lara when I grew up.

I won't be ready on time. Do I have a bag or not? I have to. I'll need at least two spare pairs of socks, a cell phone, tampons, and a card holder. I'm going to take this tiny one that goes well with the dress. Shoes. Pietro is going to be there. I can't go wrong with the shoes. Let's see, these. Beautiful, black, danceable, and painless. War underwear or peace underwear? War. I'm not a warrior, but it makes me feel secure. I haven't worn this bra yet. Now the make-up. Quick, quick, the doorbell is going to ring at any moment.

Triiiiiiiiiiiiiiiiing! Triiiiiiiiiiing! Triiiiiiiiiiiiiing! Triiiiiiiiiiiiiiiiing!

Pietro is here! The sooner I think about him, the sooner he shows up. Always on time, the beard.

–Chloé, honey, send him in and give him a coffee! And don't let him be in a hurry, make-up is an art!

Patience is also an art. Didn't you want etiquette? Let's see what etiquette is. Let's see. Clinique, Sephora, Lancôme... Is that a pimple? No. Phew. The last thing I need is a pimple in addition to my periods. If there were remote-makeup artists, this would be an ideal time to make a phone call. Chloé is already opening the door.

–Hello, Chloé. I was fortunate. There was a parking space right outside the door. I think I'll leave the car here and we'll take a cab. I don't know about the Scala area with all this partying.

–Wow, what a difference! This afternoon, you looked like the German beggar at the Duomo, and now a gentleman! If I didn't know your dark side from Lucia, I would ask myself questions.

–Just look at the novice! I see you've already smoked a couple, haven't you?

–I don't need THC to form my opinions, little piece of shit. Thank me for the compliment so as not to stain the first impression and come in. I'll get you a coffee. Lucia is almost ready.

–Lucia! We're not dating anymore! You don't need to make me wait! I'm kidding! You don't need to get mad either!

This one will never grow up. What a pain in the arse! I can't lose my concentration now. If my mascara runs, I won't get out of here in half an hour. Perfect. Now the new dress. *Voilà*! I'm going to make an entrance. Let's see the mirror. Better than I thought.

–Well, what do you think?

They take a long time to respond. I'm ready for the Duomo or the Oscars. Pietro is the first to speak.

–I'm at a loss for words, little one. In the store, I couldn't imagine such a result. You look beautiful, princess.

–You're looking good—both of you. Let's see if you'll come back the same. You'll end up more like a pair of towels, and each one of you will go your separate ways. I want to take a picture of you. Just a second, and I'll get the camera.

–Thanks, guys. Hey Pietro, how are we doing? I think we should take a cab.

–We're taking a cab, yes. Anyway, we're not so bad on time. Did you get that pretty for the Spaniard? I'm going to be jealous.

–You take care of Brazil. I'll take care of my own business. I dress like this for me. Has Mommy give you her blessing and kiss you goodnight? Do you have a time limit, Cinderella?

–Don't mess with mom. We were doing very well. Besides, she loved you very much. You know that.

–Yes. Seeing me impaled in the Colosseum is what she wanted. Come on, smile for the camera. You're already decent. Hands off, you pig. You've had your share in your time. At your age, you should be ashamed to go on living with your mother.

–You are wrong. We only share a landing. And the door that connects the two floors is always closed.

–Yes, it's always closed, except for that day when you insisted on playing Basinger from *Nine and a Half Weeks*. I almost lost my face in shame. And the bitch, instead of leaving discreetly, dared to stay there to give you morale. Come on, Leo. Please don't sell me shoes. It's been so many years. How can you claim independence if the whole building is hers? And he has others. You could have at least gone to another one, couldn't you? Or to Como's house.

–Mom is very old, and she looks forward to having dinner with her firstborn from time to time. Don't go on. She's a poor widow. Since Dad died, she's been bored out of her mind.

–Well, look. You are the widow's son. You can be a Freemason.

–How nice…

Chloé takes two pictures of us. I drink my coffee in one gulp, and off we go. A cab ride together and then each sheep with his partner. Our story was very nice, and I still like Pietro, but I got rid of a good one.

8 Via Giorgio Pallavicino

I am forty-three years old and still live with my mother. I don't have a formal girlfriend since Lucia and I broke up. I haven't had much time either. Between work trips, the bloody Chinese factory, and the hotel's purchase in Malta, I can't get enough. I think Malta is going to be a good deal. It is the second line of cliffs, but according to the geologists' team's studies, the sea will have done its job in twenty years, and it will become the first line. In all that time, we will have already amortized the current purchase, and we will even be halfway to pay off the financing for the purchase of the third line. Few deals are done like this anymore. It's all taken care of. If I don't hurry up and have children, Stefano's children will keep everything, and they are capable of polishing it off in ten years... They are quite capable, no doubt about it. My little brother is a great one. He has them well under control in the American boarding school. Ok, he's the youngest, but he could have swallowed some of the stuff from China.

What happens is that there are no values anymore. Dad was right. I have fewer and fewer left, but my little brother goes beyond the limits. We had agreed on a year's vacation each to manage things, and he already owes me two with the excuse that I'm not married, and he is. I'm going to take three in a row because of China. I'll be damned! Today I'm going to put on my red tuxedo to see if I can get over my anger.

I have to pick up Lucia at half past ten. I'm going to have dinner with mother. Antonietta told me today she has pomegranates with wine for dessert. I'm sure she said that to me following the instructions of the lady of the castle. I know my cattle well. Let's see the tuxedo. It's impeccable. I'm going to match last year's patent leather to this one. They'll say I'm going as a traffic light. I hate black tie parties. If they only knew what it takes to show off without making a fool of yourself. Just ask Prince Charles. Well, all in order.

–Hello Antonietta, where is the lady?

–Your mother has been sitting naked in the closet with the door open for half the afternoon. Try to convince her to close the door, Master Pietro, it's very unpleasant. We are not monkeys, are we? Why do I have to see her like this and listen to her misfortunes? I get paid to clean and cook.

–Hahaha! You know her, Antonietta. She's afraid of being locked up, and at her age, she doesn't take orders. Don't worry, come on. I promise you that we've almost convinced her to hire two professional nurses around the clock. Her stomach doesn't let her live anymore.

–May God hear you, sir. Please don't laugh. We're going from bad to worse. Would you like to try the chestnut soup? It's just the way the Duke liked it. God rest his soul. I think I'm the only one who misses your father.

–We all miss him, Antonietta. Even madam proves it by constantly railing against him. Excellent soup Antonietta, dad would be delighted.

Poor Antonietta is right. Mom is of the old guard and has never known what empathy is. Since she became a widow, she can get downright unbearable. When she loves you, it's even worse. She adores me, and every time I hold her close, it's like the sound of a rusty hinge. I think I've only ever seen her give kisses to newborns. One day, Antonietta gives her soup with surprise. I have to convince her about the nurses urgently.

–Mom, Are you there?

–Come in, son, come in. Let's see if you can help me clean myself up. I don't look good. Have you closed the day doing the same stupid things you always do, or have you managed to lower your average?

–For God's sake, Mom. It's not going to be the end of the month before I hire nurses. You look terrible. You can't go on like this! And please close the bedroom door with a lock. The commissioner told me that the number of rapes of old women in the neighborhood has increased.

–There will be no nurses! I'm perfectly well on my own! I'm not going to be instructed by a pushover of your stature.

–Oh, yeah? Well, look, you're going to dress yourself today. If you don't get your blouse buttoned, they'll be here on Monday. I'll wait for you in the dining room.

–Are you testing me? I'll show you the dignity of our Sardinian kind. Go to the dining room, unnatural son, and go to hell too! I'll take care of myself!

Antonietta is as right as rain. I'm going to the table to read the headlines, to see what the world is saying. Let's see. Yes. The world says what it always says. Most journalists' lousy thing is that they believe everything they think and then write it in headlines. What a force the Brazilian has. That night in Florianopolis I had a hard time forgetting her swagger. Sandra, how well the pink *tailleur* looked on her, despite her horrendous shoes! I'd like to know how the absence of a dress suits her. Here comes Mom with her head held high. She's managed to fasten three buttons out of ten and hasn't sleeved her sleeves.

–Come on, Mom, come here. Three buttons aren't wrong at all. You look like a champ. Just a second. Tuck your right arm in here, very good. The other one, great. Mom, I'm going to spend the whole next month at the lake house. Do you want me to tell Stefano to come to stay with you?

–If he doesn't come to see me on his own, don't tell him anything at all. Hey, squirt, are you going to the lake? You could hire someone to help me in your absence.

–Of course, Mom, if that's what you want, that's all there is to it. Ring the bell and call for dinner. I'm in a hurry. I'm going to a party tonight.

–Thanks son, you're useless, but at least you're not too much of a nuisance.

I did it! It will cost a bundle for the nurses, but now they won't leave the house until the Greek calends. Of course, I have no intention of going up to the lake. It takes at least a week to warm up there, and it's too barren to go alone.

–Hey, mom, did you like Lucia, or didn't you like her?

–What questions are you asking me! To have a foolish son, we'd rather had the Russians come to put the grandparents to the sword, as they did with poor Nicholas and his daughters. I have raised you so that you fill my house with commoners? And no less than a Sicilian, daughter of two thousand kinds of milk! But what do you think? If you wanted an answer, here it is. Bad blood. Bad blood as all the poor girls that have crossed that threshold.

–Well, Mom, how exaggerated you are. I think you're the only fascist with your tongue out that's still alive in Italy. I know quite a few of them. Quite a few. You should have seen the last club meeting. Hey, how does Antonietta's chestnut soup turn out? I think I'm going to take her to the lake—Antonietta, not the soup.

–You take Antonietta to the lake, and I don't respond to my acts! What do you think you're doing? As long as I'm breathing here, you do what I say. Lazy, lazy, and without any respect! How you remind me of your father's lazybones, you only lack the vice of gambling.

She's on fire. It's perfect. That's how she thinks best. I'm going to ask her about China, let's see what she thinks. I admit that the Spanish issue has piqued my curiosity and, if Stefano doesn't come soon to take care of the shoes, he's going to find some last-minute surprises.

—Mom, what do you think of the Chinese? Do you think they'll buy our shoes? Giorgio is determined that we close Genoa and dump it there.

—Son, I'm glad you asked me, and look, I have an opinion for you that I've been holding back all these decades. Zurich lasts? That's a lot of nonsense. You would do well to leave them to your brother. The shoe business? Two silly things. It's not worth risking your life going from one plane to another to have the four bastards on duty wearing our coat of arms on their feet. Don't forget that selling leather is a merchant thing. Formerly, the family did this as a hobby and had the royal house's seal, which gave other royalties. Do you see a royal house anywhere in our ravaged peninsula? Neither do I. For me, you can burn all your factories!

—Mom! You're raving! I can't believe I'm hearing what I'm hearing!

—Don't interrupt me, I haven't finished, you weakling! It seems unbelievable that you are the fruit of my loins. What a shitty race! The only one who's barely saved is your sister. Mostly because she's a woman. Listen well, fool, because I won't tell you twice. I don't have long to live, but I can't leave without you hearing this. You asked me about China. It's the only intelligent question you've asked me since you were born. Money is an entelechy, Pietro. That's why blood force matters much more than money. Money has never been important. You have what the system accepts as good, but alas, if the system changes. The Chinese invented the banknote, and we adopted it right away because it wore out even faster. Today it hardly exists anymore because you have put everything in microchips. Look how little money is worth. And, since everything that will be produced in the next twenty years is already committed in the futures markets, it is worth less than nothing. Hardly a promise that always hangs in the balance. China has not lost its roots, and that makes them wiser. They are like the Church, which has the promise of eternity and the patience of the Chinese. When you negotiate with a priest or a Chinese person, you are not dealing with the person in front of you. You are negotiating with the whole future church or the entire future China.

–I'm sure the priests are aware of what you say, but I don't think that's the case with the Chinese, *mamma*.

Pietro, each Chinese, is a dragon scale, and the dragon is in no hurry. It is frolicking and laughing at our vision of the world. We, Westerners, are frantic, we want immediate results, and that is our weakness. We think we are the Trojan horses, and in reality, they lure us into their nest like the spider. But they are not going to exterminate us, nor do they want to prove anything to us. Our only job as Europeans is to convince them that authenticity is priceless. They have to keep seeing us as exotic, and then we will get our culture to survive. Leave the rest to the Americans until they learn their worth. They have more Eiffel Tower replicas planted than oil wells, and they think they can turn a Chinese into something other than a Chinese. You must always look to the past to see the future. If you want food for thought, ask yourself what has happened to all the gold that has come out of the ground in all the history of man. It is a lot of gold and has to be somewhere. And also, ask yourself what it is for. The bank will have money in its coffers, but you have to look for wealth elsewhere, son. Think also about the mechanism of the traditional fortunes and that of the neo-fortunes of your Internet. In the end, your Internet is nothing more than a colossal taximeter. Think long and hard about this, you knucklehead. Only by using your brains will you perhaps one day be able to live up to your last name, the real one, not the fake one you carry.

–You're great, Mom. I don't agree on everything, but I promise I won't stop thinking about your perspective. Very enriching. You always shed new light on things when you're not slapping me around.

–You're nothing but a fuck of mine! If I say "shit", you must answer "present"! What's for dessert, Antonietta?

–Pomegranates with wine, ma'am, as agreed.

–You and I didn't agree on anything. Go to the kitchen and get dessert!

–What a surprise, Mom, my favorite dessert! Come and let me kiss you on the forehead.

–Oh! Let me loosen your bow tie a little. You look like a butler. If my favorite wasn't your brother, how well we would get along. You know that, don't you?

–Of course, Mom. I love you too.

Mom is one of those people you have to dig to find, like a prickly pear. If you get past the thorns, you find a golden heart. She loves to speak in parables because of her fondness for priests, and you have to be very trained to know where her intentions are going. His older brother is a priest and lives two floors below us.

This building has retained many things from the glory days, including the basement chapel. Yes, Mom doesn't need to go to church except for weddings, baptisms, and communions. She has the parish priest and altar at her home, and when we were kids, there was no way to get away for a single Sunday or feast day.

She has also always had one of the apartments rented to a French hairdresser—a very funny man with a Salvador Dali-like mustache and very long hands. One Sunday a month at home has always been a haircut for the whole family. Even for the service staff.

–Well, Mom, I'm leaving, I'm late. If you need anything, call me, I'll have my cell phone on.

–I won't call you even if I'm suffocating in the bathtub, son. I am an independent woman. Your asshole father knew that when we got married. What's this party you're going to?

–It is the anniversary of a newspaper. The *Giornale del Mondo.* I think it will be fun.

–That reds pamphlet? I hope you don't get any ideas from them. Reds are toxic. You've chosen the color of the suit very well. Go on, have a good time, you pushover.

I go down in the elevator while I fasten my coat and put on the vicuna gloves my sister gave me last Christmas. They are beautiful. Carlota seems to have inherited the family's eye for leather. She lives in Rome and is a theater actress. I sit behind the wheel of my '81 Morgan and head for *Viale Bligni* to pick up Lucia, just like in the old days. What has changed is that I'm thinking of Sandra. Sandra and my mother's speech that has left me in one piece. This is the second time today that I hear talk of getting rid of the lasts from Zurich. Either everyone has gone crazy, or there is change floating around.

What luck I've had parking! The car stays here. Old Pasquale is where I left him, doing crossword puzzles on his porch and smoking his worn hornpipe. Even today, he would still be able to walk blindfolded to Lucia's house following strawberries' smell.

–*Buona sera*, don Pasquale How is your crossword going?

–Signore Scandia, it's been a long time! Don't tell me that you and Miss Lucia are reconciled? What good news!

–No, Don Pasquale. There is no reconciliation. Love dies, and the old friendship remains. You know how these things are.

–No, *signore*. I no longer know how these things are or any other. This world we are living in is far away from me. If it weren't for the crossword puzzles and my faithful Carola, who gives me more trouble than a toothache, I don't know why I'm still here. Oh, Lord! When will the Lord take me away?

–I see you like a bull, don Pasquale. It seems you still have a lot of crossword puzzles ahead of you.

–You are very kind, *signore*. I see you as a hussar of Pavia. It's a pity you're not together. The young lady doesn't like solitude at all. She says hello whenever she passes by but rarely stops to talk to this old man. She wasn't like that before.

–Don't worry, Don Pasquale. A woman like that won't stay alone for long, you'll see. Anyway, don't forget that she's Sicilian. If she still greets you, you have nothing to worry about. I'm on my way up.

–You have a subtle Lombard humor, *signore*. Come up, come up. You are always welcome here.

9 Chloé

Chloé lived in Bordeaux with her parents. He was a winegrower, and she was a dentist. Marc and Claude. For the past two years, they had fought hard to bring their only daughter out of her "recursive asynchronous grief", as diagnosed by the third specialist taking care of Chloé. Common grief, Dr. Pillon said, is composed of four phases, namely:

The impact phase: Disbelief at the loss. Confusion, loss of appetite, nausea, and insomnia.

The guilt phase: Acceptance of the loss. Anguish and generalized emotional disorder.

The withdrawal phase: Search for the absent person. Isolation, auditory hypersensitivity, pulling in the stomach and throat, choking, and dry mouth. Sporadic hallucinations with the deceased.

The restructuring phase: Reintegration into the world and healing. Awareness, acceptance of absence, and remission of all physical and psychological symptoms.

The problem, according to Pillon, was Chloé's twelve years and her remarkable sensitivity. According to him, it seemed as if Chloé, upon reaching the middle of the third phase in an accelerated manner, was settling back into the first phase, entering a never-ending loop. She also presented other physical symptoms whose presence was not justified: panic attacks and muscular spasms very similar to epilepsy, among the most notorious. For this reason, Claude had reluctantly agreed to hospitalize her four days a week. To trace these anomalies, she was subjecting Marc and Claude to interrogation sessions that Claude seemed more like the Holy Inquisition's torture chambers. Claude was starting to become unbalanced herself and was on the verge of a nervous breakdown. Marc was doing his best to keep his temper.

–Doctor, it is not possible that there is no improvement with our daughter. You have been with her for eleven months, and your sessions with us are immoral and inhuman. I have nightmares about your pen almost every week! If this keeps up, I'm going to have to commit myself and my daughter! - The doctor imperceptibly put his pen back in his desk drawer as he resumed his verdict.

–Look, Mrs. Duthil, your daughter's case is unusual. If we don't improve in the next month, I'm considering electroshock and cold showers. Please excuse the coldness, but sometimes the classics show themselves to be of some use, and we are running out of ideas - Claude stood up in an attempt to grab the quack by the neck. She just grabbed the lapel of his dressing gown.

–That's out of the question! You're worse than your patients!? Electroshock to my little girl! And a cold shower! Marc, I'm not going through with this! And Chlo even less! - She said, turning to her astonished husband, who hadn't uttered a word for half an hour.

–My dear, please calm down. Doctor Pillon said a month, and he's probably exaggerating, aren't you, Doctor? Pillon separated Claude's hand from his lapel as gently as possible while staring at her.

–Mrs. Duthil. I must give you my scholarly opinion. We would never do anything without your consent. I beg you to consider all options at the risk of seeing your daughter stagnate in her illness and throw away her entire youth and yours.

Claude burst into a long sob and fell back in her chair. Marc did not know what to do. He looked alternately at Pillon and his wife. It seemed incredible to him that the death of a schoolmate, no matter how much of a "boyfriend" he was to his adored little daughter, was breaking down their home in this way. He grabbed both of his wife's hands and whispered in her ear.

–Let's talk it over with the little one, Claude. Chlo is suffering, but you know very well that she is not stupid. You'll see, my love, we'll get out of this, be patient - she turned her head towards Pillon -. We're taking the child to the country for a week, doctor. I suppose it won't be inconvenient for you.

–Not at all, Mr. Duthil. I'm going to fill out your release form. This is not prison, you know.

Marc told himself that it was the closest thing he had ever seen in his life if it wasn't jail. The doctor took his pen out of the drawer and concentrated on the paperwork. The room was in semi-darkness, adding a cloud of sadness to the long-suffering couple's mood. Through the window was an inner courtyard without a single bus, only reinforced concrete. It was raining heavily.

They arrived at the hospital room where their daughter lay in bed with a vague look on her face. In the neighboring bed, a lady in her seventies was snoring like a tractor. While Marc dressed the girl and sweetly told her about the country vacation he was projecting in his head. Claude collected the clothes from the locker. Marc didn't know if Chloé was listening to him because she was staring at an indeterminate point on the ceiling and didn't react. She let herself dress like a rag doll. He had become accustomed to talking to her like that when she entered these phases of absence. The first few times, he felt very uncomfortable because it was akin to talking to an unconscious person, waiting for a part of her to be processing the information. At this, the lady woke up heavily.

–Have they already taken her away? What a pity! Your daughter is an angel, gentlemen. Since she's been in my room, I've been able to digest my food.

–She is an angel, indeed, - answered Claude, troubled - Why are you here? - The lady threw the blanket over her shoulder and turned against the wall.

–My husband died last month. Since his funeral, I am not even able to get up to go to the toilet. I have no children, and I have been living in grief ever since. When my sister asked the firemen to break down the house's door, I had not eaten or drunk for almost four days, hiding under the kitchen table, and I had done everything on myself. They say I could have died of dehydration. I wish I had - she let out a deep sigh.

A shiver went up Claude's spine. She thought that if someday she was the one in the lady's shoes, at least she did have her daughter. The possibility of not recovering from her illness made a spare tear run down her cheek. She swallowed, wiped her cheek, and said goodbye to the lady, patting her shoulder.

–Courage. You will see how time will do its work - the lady slightly moved the fingers of the hand peeking over the sheet.

Claude took his daughter in his arms, and the three of them walked to the car. He spent the whole way fixing his eyes on the small, deep turquoise eyes of his Chlo, wandering blindly in Marc's footsteps through the hospital. How fast his little girl had grown! She already weighed as much as a piece of office furniture full of books. Claude was quite athletic. She had been a swimmer when she was young. She remembered with tenderness her nine months of pregnancy. She could not have any more children. When she had been given the bad news, she hadn't minded too much. Now she regretted having thought so.

They wasted no time. They were both on the phone making arrangements with their friends and colleagues for the unexpected vacation. They made reservations at a little hotel on the outskirts of Libourne, where the two of them had been going since their marriage. While Claude was packing his bags, Marc was looking for pony rides on his computer. They got into the car and entered the ring road. At this, Chloé opened her mouth.

–Can we stop at a church, Mom? - She rarely came out of her apathy.

–Of course, Chlo, why do you want to stop in a church, my love? Marc, there is a presbytery in Arveyres. My cousin Jeanne lives very close and brings cakes every week to the priest. We can stop for a moment, I'm sure it's open, and they can inform us.

–I want to pray, Mom. You don't mind, do you?

How could they care? Although he understood his daughter's question, and although they had agreed to put her in catechism class at Grandma Flore's insistence, both parents were openly agnostic. That was the only thing they agreed on. Marc was a socialist and had been a faithful follower of Mitterrand throughout his office term, while Claude voted to the right. In all other thought and philosophy chapters, they always disagreed, but they had such a fluid relationship that it did not affect their coexistence.

Chloé spent the whole ride looking out the window, but her parents sensed something was up. It was the first time they had heard her humming since her little friend's accident. They looked at each other with a knowing expression and didn't stop until they reached the presbytery, which Marc had located on his GPS.

It had stopped raining, and the floor at the entrance of the presbytery was completely flooded. They rang the doorbell, and the parish priest came to answer. He wore the unmistakable collar on his black shirt that contrasted with his threadbare jeans and boots that looked like they had just come out of a cowboy movie.

–Good afternoon, Father. Look, sorry to bother you, but our daughter asked us to stop at a church to pray, and we decided to stop here, - Marc said. - We are on our way to Libourne. The little girl is going through a severe trauma - this last, almost in a whisper, so as not to be overheard by Chloé.

Marc's hair stood on end at the mere presence of the collar at such close range. He couldn't bear the thought of seeing that the catechism had influenced his Chlo in this way, although he couldn't help thinking that, if it would somehow get her out of her vicious circle, he would swallow whatever there was to swallow. The image of electroshock was even more disgusting to him.

Claude held Chloé's hand. Somehow it was the same for her as it was for Marc, but for different reasons. She had studied with the nuns in Paris and had unpleasant memories. Without having suffered any unpleasant chapters, she did not have good memories, and she was suspicious of church people, of any church.

–Well, I have no office today, and they are cleaning the chapel, - answered the priest in boots, - but that does not impede at all if what the girl wants is to pray - he rubbed Chloé's head - What is your name, little girl?

–My name is Chloé, Father. But my parents call me Chlo. Won't I be able to pray, Father?

–We'll fix that right away, young lady. I am Father Jean. Which do you prefer, Chloé or Chlo?

–If my parents tell me, I prefer Chlo. If others tell me, Chloé.

–Then I'll call you Chloé, okay? Come on, come on, I'll show you three my house. Are you going to the lyceum, Chloé?

–I haven't been there for a long time because I'm sick. A teacher comes to my house to give me lessons. I want to pray because I want to ask God if I am going to be cured. You understand, don't you?

–Of course, I understand, Chloé, how could I not if I talk to him every night? But I never tell anyone. He said to me in a dream that someone like you would come here. Do you go to catechism, Chloé?

–When I was in high school, yes. I don't understand many things, but I like it. In my class, only two girls have made communion. I have a friend who did Bat-Mizvah this year. Do you teach catechism, Father?

Chloé had gone ahead of her mother, and, as they all walked through the garden, the parents watched in amazement as their daughter held the parish priest's hand as naturally as they spoke. The scene was becoming surreal to both of them.

They entered the priest's residence. The decor was very sparse, as it befits such places in rural France. There was a lot of junk in the entryway, including a gutted Gibson *LesPaul,* and some car parts were strewn about aimlessly. The priest set them up in the kitchen.

–I hope you like red tea. The coffee pot broke down a month ago, and I haven't had time to buy another one. I have some delicious ones brought to me every week - Claude couldn't help a slight smile. She put an index finger to her lips, asking her daughter to be quiet.

The tea will be perfect, the cakes too. Thank you very much, father – Marc said.

Father Jean began to talk about the goodness of the conventual pastry. While he was preparing the tea, he told them the anecdote about why it was customary for cloistered monasteries to be close to wineries. Marc did not know it, even though he had been involved in the world of wine all his life.

–In the past, the nuns only needed the yolks for their cakes and sold the whites to the wineries. They used them to filter the wine in the vats. Today there are very few wineries that still use this method. Fortunately, the nuns are still making commendable cakes. These are secular. How do you like them? I have a real vice. God forgive me - Chloé was already on her third.

–They are delicious, - she said with her mouth full.

–Well, Chloé, - said Father Jean. - Now, if it's all right with you, we'll both go to my emergency altar. I have it set up on the desk. If you want, I'll confess you there, and then you can stay there and pray for as long as you want, is that all right with you?

–Okay. Thank you very much, Father Jean. I'll leave my coat here - his parents nodded, he took off his jacket, and they both went to the desk, the priest reassured them with a hand gesture.

Father Jean's desk was as cluttered, if not more so than the foyer. It was a drawer of bizarre and unrelated objects. A Mexican souvenir hat from Cuernavaca, some gaucho's boleadoras, three boxes of tools, a vast collection of comic books on a chipboard shelf. On the wall was a huge painting that was a collage of vans photos seen from behind and whose license plates indicated that the photographer must have kept at least three passports full of stamps. To the right was an old stone fireplace, apparently deactivated. On its plinth rested a bright red velvet cushion, and a wooden mantelpiece covered the lintel with a statue of the virgin child and a bloodied Christless crucifix. Father Jean lit a candle at the base of the fireplace and said to Chloé.

–Well, young lady, here is everything you need. Anyway, the Lord is everywhere, and whatever prayer you have in your head, He will always listen to it. Do you want to confess?

–Yes, Father. I haven't been to Mass for a long time, and I've already lied so often that I can't take communion.

The priest took a rosary on the table, made the sign of the cross on his forehead while mumbling a litany, and began to listen to Chloé's story.

It was a long time before the priest returned to the kitchen. In all that time, Marc and Claude stood silently sipping their tea. When he returned, they both turned around anxiously.

–What did he tell you, father? I don't know if you've noticed, but we're desperate about our daughter.

–What Chloé, who is a brilliant girl, told me is a secret of confession and, seeing that you send her to catechism class, I suppose you can understand this perfectly well. However, I will have to give you some news that I don't know how much you will like.

They were a bit disoriented. So many tribulations were spoiling their temperance. They both opened their eyes in a gesture of attention.

–I have seen your daughter's case on a few occasions. Ordinary people, even specialists, cannot conceive that the sense of loss that a person of that age can go through is much greater than that of an adult. Your daughter is more affected by what has happened to her than you could ever be by the death of a loved one. I get the impression that you are not religious, am I right? - his gaze was directed towards Marc. Claude answered.

–No, father. We are firmly agnostic. You are right.

The priest clasped his hands together, resting his thumbs between the orbits as if he were praying in turn. He reflected for a few seconds and made up his mind.

–Look. I don't have to lift a finger to evangelize you. You are all grown-up and responsible adults. On the other hand, I know you are going through a tough time and don't need any more stress than you already have. You have knocked on my door, and I must give you my opinion. Value it as you wish - she looked at the frantic mother -. Your daughter will develop a profound religious vocation soon, and, in my experience, this is the best salvation plank you will find to bring her out of that state. I will leave you the contact information of a missionary who already knows these cases and will gladly take care of her when the time is right. Chloé is still very young and, no matter how hard they tried, no ecclesial authority would give her permission to begin the road to marry God. I insist, do what you want, but if you love your daughter, do nothing to turn her away from the path she is going to take, almost without realizing it. In moments of most significant doubt, check to see if her physical symptoms do not subside when she comes closer to the Lord.

–Did she tell you she wanted to be a nun? - Claude could not believe it. Marc was on the verge of collapse.

–No, ma'am, nothing like that. I am telling you that. At some point, your daughter will manifest her intention to take the habit. In a couple of years or not much longer than that. I think it's best not to take you by surprise. If I thought there was even the slightest chance of being wrong, I wouldn't risk telling them this under any circumstances. And you better never let her know about this conversation. For us, these things are science. Here are the details of Sister Odile - he handed them a card - and don't worry, I won't warn her either. Heaven alone knows how long it will take to close the circle, but it will close. Her soul has begun a path of a difficult return. We are not hucksters, as much as you may hold us in low esteem. I will pray that the Lord will give all three of you strength and that you will find the peace you crave. In the end, it is the little one that matters.

After a while, Chloé returned to the kitchen. When Claude saw her, she felt that her expression was radiant, as she almost didn't remember it anymore. She wanted to take her in her arms and put her back in her belly. The rest of the conversation was anodyne, and, with the car already in motion, Father Jean said to Marc through the window a phrase that left Chloé intrigued.

–Courage is seeking the truth and telling it. May the Lord protect you. My emergency altar will always be at your disposal, little Chloé.

Many years later, while studying political science, Chloé found the phrase that Father Jean had said that afternoon to her father in a biography of Jean Jaurès. The rest of the trip passed in silence, except for a comment from the little girl.

–Mom, Dad. I know you don't like these things, but God told me I'm going to be cured! I'm going to be fixed! Do you believe me, Mom?

–I believe you, my love, and I know it. You will be cured. You'll see.

That night, Marc and Claude did not sleep a wink.

10 Diapason

Silvia had the good habit of playing the piano in the mornings, and Jérôme had the bad habit of having mojito for breakfast on an empty stomach. He had learned it in Cuba when they met. An old man had told him that it was the best thing to have iron health, and the old man had it. The man had told him "Look, blond shrimp. If you surprise your guts with rum and lemon, nothing will be strange to them anymore. Napoleon had poison for breakfast, got it, pal?" It got on Silvia's nerves. Especially when they visited her parents and her mother was forced to put the shaker and crushed ice next to the toast.

–Are you sure you want to marry a drunken Belgian daughter? He's going to dump you as soon as he's made you a son. That is if he doesn't stay with you and does worse things.

–He's not a drunk, Mom. He takes it as medicine. You've never seen him lose his composure or babble or anything, have you? Apart from his mojito, he only drinks at parties. Besides, Jéjé is very responsible. If only you could see how fond his bosses and subordinates are of him. He has never had a single conflict at work.

–Yes. Well, for not being a drunkard, he's a good ball-buster in the morning. You know, my daughter, what do I know!

That morning was no different. Jérôme had been electric for a while with the preparation of the newspaper's anniversary, and D-Day had arrived. Silvia was rehearsing some boleros on the lounge chair, the scores of which she had downloaded from the Internet. They were the usual boleros with some exciting counterpoints. Her hands ran softly across the keyboard. The house where they lived was very ethnically decorated. Jérôme appeared through the kitchen door, mojito in hand, and just dressed in his underwear.

–It sounds very nice what you're playing today, *chérie*. - He coughed several times. His face was still puffy from sleep. Silvia was playing with passion. The night before, they had been riding on thunder for several hours.

–These are revisited boleros. I downloaded them from the web and like them very much. Are you ready for the big day, *mon petit papa?* - She hugged him up and back from her chair and kissed him on the chin. - Shave it off. You look like a hedgehog. Last night you left my neck like a minefield.

–I'm ready and in shape. I'm going to take a shower and run to the newsroom. There are still a lot of loose ends, and it's Friday. On Fridays in this town, it's not good to be in a hurry with anything, and I'm in a hurry with everything. There are a lot of things that can go wrong until midnight - he sniffed her hair -. Have a good day at the office, honey. I love you.

Jérôme drained his mojito in one sip, coughed a sharp blow to finish clearing his throat, and went into the bathroom. Silvia finished the last few chords. She closed the piano's lid and walked over to the couch to grab her purse and laptop. She noticed that it had been a while since anyone had wiped the narwhal tooth behind the piano. She put on her white Max Mara coat and went to work.

Jérôme didn't think twice. He put on an old pair of sweatpants that had been with him for several years, a pair of sneakers and a shirt with white cuffs and collar, with the old sleeve cuffs so typical of the professional printers of the thirties that he loved. Few people knew how practical the garters were for keeping your sleeves from getting too baggy when working with ink, as well as for holding small utensils or pieces of fabric or paper.

He tied a shirt-colored silk scarf around his neck in the manner of the old tangueros. The eclectic combination was his way of letting everyone who saw him know they were at *DEFCON-1*. Those closest to him already knew the code, but it caused strangeness in those who saw him appear like this, and it worked. He hung his very thin myopic glasses around his neck. He put on his Clubmasters and his everlasting black trench coat and, in turn, went to work. He also wore a black military beret shod backwards. As he picked up his envelope of Drum from the top of the tailpiece, he noted that it had been a long time since anyone had wiped his narwhal tooth.

Jérôme had always refused to get his driver's license. The Audi that the newspaper had given him was Silvia's car. He took a cab everywhere. Whenever he was asked about his private car, he always replied that the others had time to drive because they didn't have his workload. He had never had a traffic ticket in his life, of course. For short journeys, he had a notebook of graph paper that he never left, and in which he wrote down all his thoughts. During the trip to the office, he took out the notebook and wrote down all the details that would occupy him for the rest of the day.

Arriving at the Romanesque-style building where the *Giornale del Mondo* was produced, on *Via Montenapo*, as the Milanese call *Via Monte Napoleone,* he rushed like a flash to the cafeteria for his first coffee of the morning with a dry bun. Since it was Friday, he deleted his entire inbox in one scroll. Jérôme only went through his emails on Mondays, and the rest of the week, he deleted them without looking at them without mercy. He only read the SMS, which included the voice messages that came to his number. He said that email was wasting a lot of everyone's time and that the important stuff would be strong enough to pass his deletion filter anyway.

As he neatly rolled the four cigarettes that would get him to lunch, Niccolo approached his table. Niccolo was the editor, the figure that corresponds to the boatswain's mate of a warship in a newspaper's editorial office. At least that's how it was at the *Giornale del Mondo.*

–Jéjé, no can do. You've been master of ceremonies for the party all week, and you're ignoring the paper. Is there an opening for a public relations position? If so, I want to apply, and if it's you applying, then I want to apply for your position.

–If you cannot cover for me to get a decent sheet out on the street in my forced absence, who is ever going to take you seriously for my position? That's what I have you for, isn't it? Or wasn't this year's editorial line sufficiently clear at the meeting in Bari? He spat at him as he pressed the tobacco from the third cigarette with firm taps on his Patek dial.

–Very funny, Flemish, very funny. Meanwhile, my wife is already thinking about going to live with her mother if I don't start coming home at a decent hour. Luckily the party is today, and normality will return!

–Don't call me Flemish. You know I'm a Walloon. Call me Walloon if you want, *polentone*. And tell your wife to get used to it. If she wanted her husband at home, she should have married a civil servant, a politician, or an artist. We are an army. You know that. And today, we are at war.

–What damage has been done to you by your participation in "Octopus" as a cabin boy, Walloon - Niccolo took out his notebook -. Let's see, everything looks under control today, but I need to know what coverage you'll want to give the party in tomorrow's edition.

–I was not in "Octopus", dumbass. That was in the Persian Gulf in '87. I was in Rwanda in '90, and it would have been better for me not to have been there. Besides, I got a bad assignment for my famous refusal to drive, - he said, scratching his forehead. - You give the party half a page three and no more. Please don't mention it on the front page. If everything goes according to plan, we'll get coverage in all the national newspapers and quite a few abroad. - Niccolo squared his shoulders and exclaimed.

–Sir, nothing else, sir! Permission to go to work, sir!

–Dismissed! Let's see what you're up to, *mon petit père*. I hope to see you tonight. Maybe I'll consider you for the public relations position. The pubic fellatio position we'll give to your wife if you don't keep her happy.

–Very funny, sir! I wish you painful lung cancer, sir!

This verbal rudeness was characteristic of all the editorial staff and was a style that Jérôme had established. Believe it or not, women were more prone to the rant of a longshoreman than men. Some visitors came away visibly shocked. Niccolo went his way, and he went to his office. He called Teresa, his secretary, to give her instructions and see if any of the two thousand loose ends had been resolved.

Indeed, they were on schedule. The production team left the gallery ready in shape and on time, except for a couple of light cranes that had not yet been authorized to enter the town center. Teresa left the mail on the table, including a package in the French flag colors, which she guessed was carrying a compact disc he was expecting. He unpacked the box and inserted the CD-ROM into his computer. As he took his headphones out of his desk drawer, he thanked Teresa.

–Don't leave your phone lying around. It's hot today. Activity, Teresa! Today was not the best day to come with those platforms.

–Don't worry about my platforms. If I have to take them off for something, I'll take them off, you bully. Activity, blondie, activity!

-Lalalalalala. I'm not here for anyone for the next twenty minutes. For no-body.

He put on his wireless headphone and lit his first cigarette of the day as he began to move to his pad notes into his corporate agenda and opened the rest of the paper mail. The CD file was precisely what he had asked Martine for the night of the Folies Pigalle in Paris. Much better than he could ever have hoped for. He let out a howl of satisfaction.

Jérôme was a fan of classical music. He and Silvia would take advantage of their La Scala season ticket for whatever concert they could whenever they could. Martine worked at the Opera Bastille, the hideous mammoth that serves as France's musical heart in the same name's historic Parisian square. Between drinks that night, it had occurred to her that a tuning session would do very well for the first hour of the party. The brief minutes that always pass between the orchestra musicians taking their seats and the conductor's arrival. Strings, winds, brass, and percussion in apparent disorder as a prelude to the most delicate and cleanest vibrations in the world.

Martine had sent him, recorded in the highest fidelity, a whole hour of tuning that she had mixed herself in the studio of her husband, Philippe. That's what she told him in the note that accompanied the record. Indeed, she had collected the favors that the musicians of the orchestra must have owed her. She was the one in charge of managing the institutional invitations to concerts, and they were always giving her a hard time. After fifteen minutes of dynamic listening to the entire recording, which was studded with playful musical dialogues between instruments and musicians, and which converged at the end of the file on the "Emperor's Waltz", with its complete introduction, Jérôme picked up the phone and dialed Martine's number. He had it disconnected. He dialed Teresa's number.

–Teresa, open your email in five minutes. Use the scan with my signature and include the text I'm sending to you. You call the florist and tell him that I want twenty-four white orchids to arrive today at noon at the address I'm also sending to you. You say to him that if he doesn't guarantee it, we'll find another florist today and for the rest of the year. Thank you, my dear. Text me when you get it.

He then set about writing Martine's card.

"Dear rose of France, these flowers require very special care. They demand a lot of moisture and only show their best face when you insult them with the most infernal words. Tell Philou that you have earned my eternal gratitude for the recording and my admiration for the exquisiteness in the mix - a perfectly ordered chaos! I am sad not to have you around on this special evening, but this fantastic composition you send me somewhat compensates for that emptiness. See you very soon."

No sooner had he got up from his chair than three columnists came in at once, and Niccolo was still cursing at them.

–They're worse than dogs, Jéjé! Either you muzzle them, or things are going to get ugly!

–Boss, this useless guy wants to put the three of us on the second to last page of tomorrow's edition! Between the classified ads and the weather forecast! If you want, the three of us can dress up as Go-gos and have our picture taken! With your phone next to you! - Jérôme was patient.

–Let's see, guys. I'm in a lot of trouble, and this is neither Parliament nor a schoolyard. Who's in charge of this mess?

–You, boss. Of course - all four answered in unison.

If I have said that Niccolo is my substitute until after the party, this is papal infallibility. What part did you not understand?

–Chief, you know the profession better than anyone here. We're going to be a laughingstock. Give us some airtime and put us at least in the centerfolds.

–They think they're at the top of the blacklist, - Niccolo burst out, making a gesture of tearing off his shirt. Jérôme was definitive.

–There are no blacklists and no deviations of authority, period. If Niccolo has decided that you go there, there you go. However, I had full confidence in his judgment, and I haven't read you for a month. Suppose tomorrow your material isn't good enough. In that case, either you'll stay on that page until the Mistral blows down to Monte Rossa from the sea, or you'll end up lining at another paper - he pointed at each of them in turn with his glasses - Don't you understand I'm risking your jobs with the damn party? Have I been hiring morons all year? Do you want me to tell the board that there's no electricity in the box because you've had me all day with tomorrow's edition? Answer, Carlo, *mon petit père*. Don't stand there looking like a fool - the three of them looked at each other, and Carlo took the floor.

–Whatever you say, boss. Excuse me, boss. We're going to write, boss. Coffee, boss?

–Yes, thank you very much. Two lumps. Niccolo, stay a second - the three of them walked out of the door in a troubled state, and Niccolo stood there looking victorious.

–Don't look like that, Niccolo. Sending them to the penultimate position is a mistake, and you know it very well. What's wrong with all of you today? Why didn't you put them in the center?

–Their topic today is to attack German car manufacturers for the new European emissions law. You know who has given us the three full pages of advertising this quarter. I want them to go as unnoticed as possible so that it gets published without shit starting to rain down and have the party in peace under my short tenure.

–Well, I don't think it's right of you. If you have to attack, you attack, and if it hurts someone, let them talk to me. I have more cards to defend him later for having delegated to you. Sometimes you have to take a gamble, Niccolo. You have to live by taking a risk. That's what our profession is all about. To sell advertisements, there are already the commercials - he said this very convinced.

–Are you putting me as a human shield in this matter? - Niccolo blurted out indignantly.

–Well, yes, look. I'll put you as a human shield, and then I'll go out alone under the shrapnel to defend your decision. You're going to look like you've got some balls. You don't deserve me, Niccolo. Come on, don't say anything to those guys and put their plea in central. It will also look like you have a heart, *mon petit père*. And let me work in peace, I beg you. No more interruptions.

–Sir, yes, sir! Thank you, sir! - At this, Carlo arrived with the coffee.

–Two lumps, boss. Anything else I can do for you, boss? Am I interrupting something?

–No, Carlo. Niccolo was just leaving. I haven't been able to convince him to change the page, and he may be right. Whatever he says goes. Close the door on your way out - without Carlo seeing him, he winked at Niccolo.

Jérôme lit another cigarette, he was beginning to think that four would not be enough as the morning was coming. His phone rang. It was his contact at the Carabinieri headquarters returning the call he had made about the cranes.

–What's the matter, "Gargantua"? Who's on their period today? Why don't my cranes fit? - He snorted.

–It's nothing, "Blondie". Don't worry. The drivers were a little bit pissed off, and they were being fined. They didn't know about the international filming. In an hour, you'll have them in place.

–I hope you won't fool me, Roberto. Today we will leave the city's flag flying high - the code names were a joke between them. As Jérôme always said: "Here, everything is known".

–Lose care, "Blondie", everything is already underway.

As he hung up, he received an SMS from Teresa. She read it as Niccolo reappeared through the door.

–Flowers OK. Florist missed the first threat of the week. Activity Boss!

–What's the matter now? Are you going to give me a break or what? You're going to organize the next party. We won't wait another twenty years. I assure you, *mon petit père*, - Niccolo interrupted for the first time in years.

–We have the Scala, Jéjé! I just got a call from the director! They're leaving it to us until three in the morning!

–I thought I'd lost this one. With the theater stage, the imaginary news of the invited characters would be an absolute hit! He only needed to strategically install some screens in the gallery and some theater cameras to have complete diffusion in the whole gallery. The theater would be like a VIP area. If only he could convince the director to extend the hour a little more, he could have a *chill-out* in there with no volume problems.

He was most concerned about the circulators, especially the patrons of the seven-star gallery hotel, who were going to have some free access passes to get in and out of the event area. It was the best deal he had been able to get with the owners. By the time he considered celebrating the anniversary at the Galleria Vittorio Emanuele, it was too late to close the hotel at a reasonable price for that night. Even though it is accessed from the back street, they wanted to mitigate the predictable noise complaints in any way possible. He had to convince the director of La Scala to extend the hours.

For the rest of the morning, Jérôme lost count of the cigarettes he had rolled and the trips he had made back and forth between the gallery and the newspaper office. He had time to convince La Scala's director and met him, his wife, and Silvia for lunch. Together they calculated the time and resources it would take to dismantle the theater's seating to set up the VIP area with its catering and transform it into a discotheque at the appropriate time.

La Scala had fallen from the sky. Without the theater, the party would have been more like a rock concert because of the crowds. The numbers of the fortunate guests were going out, which he knew would double the number of official invitations. Teresa kept the list and was going crazy, the SMSs were coming and going, and the poor woman's right hand was completely stiff. Jérôme had already had a small callus on his thumb some time ago and was typing the messages at breakneck speed.

He spent an hour locked up with the production company manager in a room with seven whiteboards and a bucket full of markers. They went over everything down to the smallest detail. Security, the order in which the catering trays were to be taken out in each of the zones, the sound, the bars and their acrobatic cocktail experts, the emergency generators, the evacuation plan, the licenses, the changes in decoration, the artists, the cleanliness, the information leaflets, everything. The man, Giuliano, had insisted on the ice statues. Jérôme thought they were a hideous invention but agreed that some people would be amused by the idea and let it go. The production manager had hired a walkie-talkie system with very discreet headsets that would connect all the teams in a virtual cloud. He liked to call it artificial telepathy. All he had to do was give a command, and a swarm of waiters and security guards would respond as one man. Similarly, they would both be informed of what would happen at any point in the party area. Once the meeting was over, he was satisfied and decided to delegate everything to Giuliano. He would only attend to last-minute emergencies.

Passers-by peered curiously from the other side of the huge tents that covered the entrances. Some were taking pictures. There were fifteen minutes left before the lunch appointment, and Jérôme returned to the newsroom to get dressed in civilian clothes. He had a closet in his office with five complete clothes changes to be ready for any eventuality. As he dressed, he looked in the mirror and felt like he did when serving in the army. The party was taking years off him. He smiled with confidence.

11 Overture

We are arriving at the Duomo as planned. Sandra is wearing a nice off-white dress vaguely reminiscent of a senator's toga, very appropriate. We have arranged to meet at the same column, at the cathedral's door, like a few hours ago. As the two of us walk through the square, we see quite a few couples of party guests swarming around, unmistakable because they are all dressed as penguins, like me. Even though the pigeons are busy with their domestic chore, I'm scanning around us to see if any photographer is with crumbs in his fist and wanted to make jokes. I see Pietro in the distance, unmistakable, the only Stratocaster-red penguin.

–Hi guys, how was dinner? - exclaims Sandra, giving them both a kiss and standing very close to Pietro. I mimic her and discreetly follow Lucia, who is radiant. A while ago, Jéjé confirmed by SMS that we are all on the guestlist - we went to a Japanese restaurant, it was great.

–We each went our way, - answered Pietro. We had to wear long dresses. I wore the most discreet tuxedo I could find, but Lucia looks spectacular, don't you think?

–Of course, as far as I know you, I'm probably the most discreet, you silly, - Lucia replies, sticking out her chest slightly. - Do you like my new suit? *Word of honor*, I love it. What do you say, you little shrink? Psychoanalyze this!

–Pietro is right. You look wonderful. Next to you, I look like the waiter. Or the crow-wolf from before - either sake has clouded my senses, or this woman with emeralds in her eyeballs, with whom I have barely exchanged a few words, is provoking me. Without hesitation, I present my forearm to her with a helpful attitude. She grabs my arm with a smile. - We're ready, aren't we? Shall we go to the gallery?

You can hear a fascinating eclectic mix of strings and oboes playing cat and mouse from the square. This afternoon's tents covering the gallery have been removed, and white rotating spotlights frame an impressive *LED* sign with the newspaper's logo crowning the central arch and giving a touch of elegant modernity to the already elegant Milanese neighborhood.

The Vittorio Emanuele Gallery was designed by the late Mengoni, who died during its construction without seeing it completed. It is a crossroads of pedestrian streets covered by a glass and metal dome and bounded at the entrances by majestic arcades. The floor is a monumental multicolored stone mosaic. It is a pleasure to stroll around during the day, take a Cinzano bitter in their terraces, or just browse the windows in a splendid architectural ensemble in the manner of Burlington Arcade in London, which pioneered this type of design in the nineteenth century. Whoever passes through here should not fail to stomp on the testicles of the rampant white bull that presides over the armorial shield on the floor to invoke good luck, they say. The tradition may also be based on some obscure family quarrel that has passed through time to the present day. A Jewish client once told me that the Arab-Israeli conflict began because of a goat. The noble animal, completely desensitized, accuses the quaint tradition without batting an eye.

Accesses are fenced with antique railings, very much in keeping with the rest of the complex. I wonder if they were brought by the organization or are heritage of the city. Access control is tight but fluid. We just have to suffer ten minutes of the queue, and it's twenty past eleven. People are falling into the dance. I find it impressive that the newspaper has managed to close all the restaurants in the place, including the inevitable Café Biffi, from which on occasion I have staggered out due to the treacherous effect of its delicious negronis.

The decor of the party is worthy of praise. We all wonder what budget line Jéjé has moved and what surprises the evening holds in store for us. A few round balloons, several meters in diameter and completely spherical on the ceiling, provide the lighting. Along the cornices, there is a powerful, well-integrated light and sound installation. Several giant screens scattered in apparent disorder along the facades and framed in imitation gold leaf show some guests' faces, who are being interviewed by teams of journalists and filmed in depth by several cameras installed on mobile cranes throughout the gallery.

It is all decorated with comfortable leather sofas, coffee tables, plants, huge paintings of modern art, designer chairs. They have certainly worked thoroughly to exploit the nickname of the gallery, *il salotto*, which is how it is popularly known. For its size and configuration, the combination is a success. All those people dressed for the occasion, the waiters coming and going with their trays full of glasses of sparkling wine and exquisite gorgonzola and walnut sandwiches or prosciutto with dried tomato and black olive paste, the ingenious musical setting. Every turn of the head reserves to the eye a new detail full of originality.

At the entrance, we are given an informative brochure and a special edition of the first issue of the *Giornale del Mondo,* which, among many other curiosities, has as its main cover story the election of Boris Yeltsin as president of the Russian Federation. After leaving our coats in the checkroom, we make ourselves strong around a glass table with a bronze mermaid as its base, and which is located quite close to the emasculated bull, which we do not fail to visit and pay its pagan homage to with a clean heel. The space under the central dome is empty and will probably be the dance floor. The light and sound booths have occupied the second-floor rooms in two of the corner buildings, and we note that the activity is frenetic in their balconies.

The brochure contains a map of the party area with a description of the theme bars, tasting booths, the list of scheduled performances, and other security details. Inside is stapled the access card to the VIP area, which, as we learned later, was made by hand because of the unexpected awarding of the space at La Scala. Everything is very well organized and we have a long and pleasant evening ahead of us.

The girls are busy browsing through the newspaper and amusing themselves with the ads and the apartments' prices in the classifieds. Pietro and I, almost by hormonal inertia, are looking around us in an apparent hunting drift. There is a lot of beauty around. Lucia brings us back.

–Do you remember the boom of apartments at the beginning of the nineties? Well, at these prices, if I sold mine today, I would buy three of them in the town's center.

–That boom of the nineties must have been in Italy - I answer - what cries out to heaven is our case.

–If I tell you my opinion, even bread is going to go up. This one's on me - we all laughed at Pietro's oldest joke in the world. It was all for free.

–Bubbles for everyone! - says Lucia. - Give us a bubble, Pietro, let the bread rise!

–Well, but quickly, because the subject is hackneyed. It is already boring to talk about real estate's ups and downs. Today, the most painted person is an expert in the stock market, an expert in apartments, an expert in everything. How right Umberto Eco was when he was suspicious of the Internet! Look, I would not like to be in the shoes of a university student of our time.

The only option left to them is to beg for shackles. In the post-baby-boom period, one salary per family could buy the main house, a second house, a car, and a few splurges depending on the individual.

–That's more or less it, - I answer.

–I didn't exist then, and Brazil has other dynamics. But go on, go on - Pietro continues.

–Besides, back then, a university degree was good for something more than it is today, and the qualification of the incipient immigration of that time was residual - he drinks his Asti in one gulp -. Okay, guys, I'll make it short for you. We are going to witness the boom of wage renting and the Russification of the housing market. The banks have done excellent business. They are becoming the real owners of all the habitable land in the big cities, like the old feudal lords. The next decade's star product is already being hinted at: Turnkey homes in exchange for your payroll! The bank lets you choose from its broad catalog of apartments whose purchase was partially financed by the imprudent who got into the roulette wheel late and ended up in foreclosure due to non-payment. The bank is your landlord, and the first thing it deducts from your salary is the rent. First point.

–That's one way of looking at it, certainly. The second point?

–The second point is the million-dollar question: Should the banks be blamed? My answer is a resounding no. Here the Ponzi pyramid is generational. The bank is merely doing its job. It is not responsible for the client's lack of judgment, who signs voluntarily, driven by greed and fear they have been taught in their homes and their schools. If I, your father, bought two houses for 200 and I sell one of them today to your little cousin, your generation, for 300, I am already doing well. Add to that my retirement, and I'm going to make a soft landing. The bank finances your little cousin. He doesn't have the 300. The rest is all Ponzi. Me dad, I'm going to spend your next 40 years of sweat, and when you want to do the same to your son, nobody will buy land because it will all be in the hands of corporations, and individuals cannot compete with that.

–It is something crude and schematic, but it has a lot of truth - Lucia answers -. And I understand that the term "Russification" refers to joining several people in the same space to reduce costs. That's for sure. In Sicily, we have always said that bricks are not edible. As for me, I think that today, you no longer buy stone, but cubic meters of air between the walls. Walls of increasingly thinner paper. In the United States, the big business is tornadoes because the houses there are all prefabricated. The same tornado here does not make the headlines there because here nothing is as devastated. They have a cycle of tornado, rebuild, tornado, rebuild.

–I usually stay away from this topic because I think that, regardless of the position, it's all just a matter of time. And what will come will come - I intervene -. But I believe in an abrupt paradigm shift that will catch us all off guard.

–And where would the paradigm go, you crazy eater? - Lucia directs a more than suggestive cleavage at me. I drink my glass in one gulp myself.

–The paradigm is a mystery. The only certainty is that we are all doing the math, thinking that today's young people are assholes, and we are all going to be disappointed. Do you know the famous legend of the scorpion suicide?

–Yes, the scorpion commits suicide with its own poison when cornered.

–Well, it is nothing more than that, a legend. It seems to commit suicide, but it is immune to its poison. It is nothing more than a spasm. Well, that is what we are going to see. An apparent suicide spasm of the next generation, and when we turn around, we will see the sting. They will most likely invent their own model, their own needs, their own new ways of relating, their own currency, and they will show us a beautiful middle finger when we tell them that they have to continue working according to our model. And they will do good business.

—Why good business? - asks Sandra.

—We are making health care worse for our model. We are increasing the retirement age, eliminating benefits, and long etcetera to increase its agony because we do not bother to give it viable, real, and hopeful alternatives. If we are not getting better, we should look better. We give mouth to mouth to the system without plugging their lung gap and only giving them the right to pay taxes. Who is going to buy that? A generation that has bonanza as school? "Look, little one, now you have to tighten your belt for the rest of your life because the party is over, and you have to pay the bill." Let's see where the little one squeezes when they squeeze him a little bit more.

—I'll tell you that where I come from, we are more day to day - Sandra sits down again with a whole bottle of Asti for everyone -. You guys are born with your life plan stapled to your noses, and to change your plan, bombs have to fall from the sky. I would like to see you with our interest rates. By trying so hard to kill the imagination of those young people, Leo says, and among whom I include myself, of course, ideas will bloom like daisies. The jungle eats the asphalt.

–I propose that we take turns to go for a walk and see a bit of this, so we don't lose our little living room. This is starting to fill up, and they are turning up the volume. What do you think? Are you coming, Lucia? - This time, I offer her my open hand straight up. She accepts it with a soft blink of her jewels and gets up.

–So far, couple. It won't be long now. There's nowhere to get lost anyway.

Good chemistry is setting in between the two. It also seems that Sandra and Pietro are not on the wrong track. We hold hands like teenagers while I tell her about my adventures with Jéjé in Bonn, and we stop at the tasting stations. We have all just finished dinner, but there are temptations that it would be a shame to resist. The bustle of people around, the music gradually taking over, and Asti's drinks start to take their toll. She, in turn, begins to tell me about her seven-year relationship with the Duke.

Standing at a bar attended by a couple of waiters dressed in oriental attire and serving only *lychee* and *kumquat* martinis in a circus-like fashion, the musical swinging increases in power, and I recognize the first chords of the "Emperor's Waltz". Lucia also seems to recognize them instantly. We look at each other knowingly and, determined, she drags me onto the dance floor where couples are dripping little by little to the martial rhythm of the violins. The martinis are left to their own devices. It seems that we are at the center of the universe, *l'ombelico del mondo*, as Jovanotti would say. My skin bristles with a faint joy as I grab Lucia's finely tuned waist, and we begin to revolve. She, too, seems to be enjoying the palatial scene.

Strauss rocks us gently under the central dome of the *salotto* in a rite that has been repeated all over the world for two hundred years. This starter has the touch of Jéjé. I remember the conversation with Martine in Paris last month, and I do not take my eyes off Lucia, who is subjugating me more and more.

The waltz is a "potato chorus" for adults. The only fixed point in front of you is your partner. Everything else spins around. It's good to be lucky enough to like your dance partner visually because their image invades your insides as the music progresses. Almost everyone is dancing, not only on the dance floor but also among the sofas, towards La Scala, under Da Vinci's stony gaze, and the other entrances. Some guests are accomplished dancers and perform more expert turns. Screens show aerial views of the set. I hope this is being recorded. A few feet away, we see Sandra and Pietro also dancing. That red tuxedo proves quite practical.

As the final chords burst out, everyone breaks into unanimous and compact applause while the lights dim and Jéjé appears on the screens, accompanied by an elderly man. They are on the stage of the theater. Jéjé approaches the microphone and addresses the camera in his perfect Italian as the applause subsides.

"Thank you, thank you. Thank you all very much. *Merci* Martine, thank you, Silvia - he blows a kiss in the air. No doubt it is being recorded -. I am Jérôme Van der Linden, and I want to welcome you on behalf of all of us who make the *Giornale del Mondo*. A team of unblemished, or almost unblemished, professionals that I have the honor and pride to lead." The audience laughs in a murmur.

"I am not going to explain how hard the preparations have been to get to share this evening with all of you while maintaining the daily production of our newspaper at the usual level of demand. From here, I apologize to the partners and families of our collaborators who, I know, have stoically suffered their absence home for this peak of work. You are the salt that makes us put our pepper on these pages every day. A round of applause to you all".

"I have by my side our beloved founder. Everyone knows him. I had the honor, in my youth, of being his assistant and putting up with his countless manias. He also cost me a black eye in the much-talked-about Roman marijuana incident. He is the one who begged for the funds so that, twenty years ago today, we brought to light that first copy of which you have been given a dedicated replica, and which some years later secured my livelihood in Milan when Giorgio called me to fill the position I occupy today. I yield the floor to the honorable and incombustible Giorgio Tavola!"

Applause. We are all looking intently at the screens. Tavola is a very controversial and highly respected man in Italy.

12 Interlude

Mr. Tavola contrasts with Jérôme by his simple clothes and his size. He wears a plain shirt and a wool sweater. Jéjé adjusts the microphone to his height before passing it to him. The applause stretches for a long time.

Sandra and Pietro, who have already joined us, suggest that we take advantage of everyone concentrating on the speech to go to the VIP area and watch the lectures live. We head over there and see that some of them have had the same idea. In the Scala square, they improvised a bridge of aluminum scaffolding and wood from the gallery to the theater entrance to allow pedestrians and cars to pass underneath without closing the access. Very smart on the part of the production company. Of course, the bridge's agglomerate is covered by the classic red carpet and railings lined with gold fabric. We enter the theater, in whose lobby some screens show the stage. There are a lot of people, everyone is smiling, and the sparkling wine is still flowing. Tavola takes the floor. His voice tone denotes an extreme affability.

"Thank you, Jerome. I hope your notebook is up to date with the absences of some team elements for their partners. Dear strangers, it is an honor for you to have my presence today... No. Excuse the vanity. It is a great honor for me to introduce today the anniversary gala of our beloved newspaper - general laughter -. I say "our" newspaper because, since its conception, it has kept its vocation of independence and openness. A *Giornale* for everyone."

"As you have all been amply informed, after all, informing is the specialty of the house, the party starts with a little journalistic game. I ask you to show your solidarity with our illustrious guests tonight, who, without being from the media and, in some cases, without speaking our language, have given us their time for this pastime and will immediately come to this podium to read their contributions."

"Based on a fictitious hypothesis developed by Jérôme, they will take us on a walk through each of the sections, gathering material that will be expanded and edited for a special issue. Be sure to buy it on time. It will be one more souvenir of this night that promises to be magical in every way. I won't bore you any longer. I return the microphone to our dear director and wish you a splendid evening!"

Jéjé returns to adjust his microphone and put on his glasses while Tavola leaves the stage parsimoniously, waving his hand in a cordial farewell under the applause and some "Vivat! "

"Thank you, godfather. I kiss hands. If anyone resembles Don Corleone in his false parsimony, it is Giorgio. Don't be fooled by his nice wool sweater. He is still the same old tiger, but now he is much wiser. We don't see him much around the house because he's dedicated body and soul to the African continent's many ills. Thank you always, Giorgio, for still being with us and beside us".

The theater is vaguely reminiscent of the Joy Eslava in Madrid but much larger and more elaborate. After all, it is the Scala of Milan. In any case, the organization has applied itself thoroughly and has turned it into a fun space. Behind the microphone, a huge sound booth soon begins to take in turns the masters of ceremony to break the righteousness that has not yet been lost. Many dark faux panelings, black silk linings, box moldings, and sci-fi furnishings herald transformations.

"So let's start, gentlemen, to let our imagination fly. Tired as we are of the generalized bipartisanship, and in this reality of strong migrations at a global level, let me introduce you to our particular *saturnalia!*"

"We have inherited a world of war, and little by little, it seems that we are going to be able to turn it into a world of peace. Armies are becoming professionalized, and compulsory military service has practically disappeared from all first world countries while the others are following suit."

"I was in the military for a while. Since then, I have been left with a variegated idea of discipline. When we contemplate the human tides that migrate to other lands searching for a better future for their children, we are looking at the heroes of our time. Without resources, without guidance, and far from their countries of origin. In the same way, the European space has allowed the great mass of students and workers to move between countries and cultures of the old continent with an ease that did not exist before."

"Hugo Pratt, that incomparable Italian creator of Corto Maltese, a hopeless nomad, once said that the only positive thing that could be taken from wars is that people get to know each other. Today, we are going to take over from Hugo, and we are going to cross war out of that discourse, leaving us with the idea that people should get to know each other".

"Ladies and Gentlemen, today's dialectical game is nothing more and nothing less than the creation of a new political party. Welcome to the founding act of the Nomad's Party! The "Partido Nomada", the "Parti Nomade", the transnational party of all citizens residing outside their place of origin. Its slogan: "Wherever you come from and wherever you are. You now belong to were you live.". Our guests will give an overview of this non-existent party's program proposals for all areas of social life. In this philosophical drift, we will see the interesting results produced by this idea."

Jérôme pauses briefly to see the general astonishment on the faces of the few people he can see under the spotlight.

"I am a firm candidate to have the card of that party, which does not distinguish between left and right, and to join it. The first resistance is from those who are not. Do not be deceived. It is not about segregating. It is about joining. It is about replacing regionalist passion with integrating passion. It is about replacing compulsory military service with voluntary civilian service, which in many cases is now a fact. Let your children ask you: Have you ever lived abroad, Dad? It's about promoting in our children the idea that they have to go and see with their own eyes what's outside the nest."

"It is also a matter of raising our awareness and of betting on the best way to welcome those who come to see us in our land with the same insatiable yearning for learning. A channel through which each State can manage the assistance to its nomads from abroad and from within. Whether these migrants are forced by necessity or by the desire to know the world. It is a question of creating an institution without borders that works. A party that reactivates the lost enthusiasm for ideological activity. It is about exchanging politicians and professionals between nations under this new flag. It is about rigorously documenting and working on an ideology that is already vibrating in the heads and hearts of millions of citizens."

"In the end, it is a matter of everyone proving with facts that there is a vibrant planet out there waiting for us with open arms to show us the magic of diversity. The Erasmus program is a great achievement of our Europe. The Nomad Party will transfer this same mechanism to the highest spheres of management, beyond European borders and the student sphere, in an unprecedented experiment until today. Our camera crews will be doing interviews with you throughout the evening so that you can enrich us with your ideas and impressions."

At this point, people began to applaud. There are many faces of doubt and, as Jéjé would later tell me, at this critical moment, he had not left things in the hands of fortune. Thanks to the wireless system of "artificial telepathy", the entire production team acted as *maître d'claque*, that classic theater character who knows the play's turning points inside out and elicits applause from the audience at the right moment. Applause, laughter, and terror are terribly contagious. I applaud following the shockwave without having finished processing the Giornale del Mondo's novel foray's imbrications. A party of expatriates. Pietro, without stopping clapping, leans towards me.

–I like your friend. It's the riskiest and most subversive proposal I've heard in years. If I were the mayor, whom I greeted a while ago, I would already be ordering the event to be shut down. Without exaggeration, under the disguise of the game hides a compelling idea, and with the best news coverage you could wish for! From the Scala stage! From the hand of Tavola! Delicious! The speakers are going to be in for a treat. The Belgian is betting big, and he seems to know it. The good thing for him is that I don't see any cobblestones or rose petals around here, just trays of impeccable Asti.

The first speaker is a well-known Caribbean singer based in Miami, very sensual by the way, who bases her speech on the parallels between the mega benefit concerts and a few original points for a hypothetical ministry of culture that would specialize in the art of fusion. Of all those he cites, I am left with the undersecretariat to exchange professors between universities and its program of points for these professionals based on services rendered abroad. He mentions in his talk a few records of mixed styles that today are best sellers.

Good for Jéjé. He has quickly moved from the rallying climate to the cultural smoothness of the hand of an international rock star who, before leaving the stage, sings his latest mega-hit.

Attention is maintained in the audience, and the interview teams are busy assailing people with questions, giving preference to the corridors that stop looking towards the stage. The orchestration is ingenious and fluid. Jéjé has so far managed to keep from emitting his characteristic guffaw. If he tells me all this in Paris, I will sell him a zero-price consultancy as long as I was present at the organization.

The political and economic program is the main focus. Two parliamentarians of the Union have been invited for this purpose. In this case, the performance is no longer a monologue but an electoral debate. The guests discuss the hottest topics of current Italian affairs, and Jéjé asks them for their opinion on their program's points related to what they are talking about. It is enjoyable because Jéjé forces them in each topic to put themselves in the shoes of the nomad who lives or is passing through Italy and who suffers the situation so that the speakers themselves contribute improvements and adaptations to the initial points of the program.

Benigni: So you believe that raising the retirement age is in the country's best interest?

Di Lucca: Ours is a contributory system; if we do not act, there will be no more circulating funds in five years, and we will have to increase taxes or drastically reduce contributions.

Benigni: Of course, you realize that this will delay access to employment for newcomers. Your measure is an unemployment enabler that also generates additional costs.

Van der Linden: Gentlemen, I refer to the following point of my party's program: "The state will assume the social security contributions as if they were treasury bills and therefore guarantees the overall value of the individual's contribution. Decisions on raising the contribution age or switching to a fully private pension system shall be submitted to a referendum among citizens with more than ten full years of contributions, as shall the right to receive a retirement pension. Community arbitration will be requested to compensate for imbalances between countries by guiding with incentives to private investment." You will understand that we will not let these limits be touched today without our permission and be touched again forever using the contributory system's argument.

Di Lucca: That is full-blown populism, if I may use the term. Life expectancy has increased, and we have to have a sustainable system.

Van der Linden: Sustainable on what basis? The state spends revenues irresponsibly and says it cannot pay pensions. Yes, life expectancy is increasing, and so is the available labor force. The State cannot employ that labor force and make the aging population pay for it.

Benigni: Then the rational thing to do would be for the State to cut costs and fully recognize its inability to manage pensions. It acknowledges that it cannot guarantee the return to the contributor of a lifetime of taxes. Since, moreover, the State has lost its ability to issue currency, we have to ask its nomads to seek employment elsewhere. Frankfurt issues the money, let it take care of the pensions.

Van der Linden: I am adding this point about centralizing Europe's pensions to the program right now; thank you. You are right about the issue of currency as a regulatory instrument. My nomads, as you say, surely include people from your family who work in England or Ireland, do not forget that, Mr. Deputy.

Di Lucca: A direct compensation system between the candidate for retirement and a family member working, with bilateral agreements between countries if the child works abroad. This way, what the grandchild is paying goes directly to the grandparent without entering the contribution wheel.

With the debate, the audience begins to take sides with howls of protest and approval. The theatrical approach helps to keep the tone relaxed, and we are all having a great time. A real debate is never the same thing as a staged provocation while you're wearing a bow tie and an open bar night ahead of you. Still, some messages get through, and we hear a lot of jokes around us. We are already quite agitated with the Asti, and it's only half past one in the morning. Sandra is having the most fun of the four of us.

–If my father sees this, his teeth will grow back! The only taxes he has ever paid in his whole life are those levied by the State on beer until it reaches his hands. And I don't even want to tell you about the pension he gets. Only zeros on the left and none on the right! You Europeans are so funny! Do you want Daddy State to pay for your manicure every week too? Then I'll tell you about the life that can be given to a check note in Brazil. You could make a soap opera with the life of a Brazilian check note!

It is true that in Brazil, checks are exchanged between individuals like school cards. They also use the qualities of inks and paper so that the documents erase themselves. I learned this on my return from a trip with some ATM receipts. There we live in the present, and here we don't, but we are all, each in our way, guinea pigs of our own lives. The most complete *Tamagotchi* ever invented is in front of the mirror. What I have not yet discovered is which of the two models is more accurate. I guess the wise thing to do is to use the best of each of them.

The debate comes to an end without any casualties, and an American basketball player takes the stage to present the program from the sports world point of view. His speech is in English, and he must be very popular because he gets a lot of applause. He must also have eaten a lot of jelly as a child because the microphone does not go higher than his chest, and the man holds it Freddie Mercury style. At this point, I hear my name behind me.

–Leonardo, good to see you! How was your day? - It's Marco who, as far as I can see, hasn't let go of negronis since this morning.

–Hello Marco! Good to see you too. I see you don't want to mix alcohols and the third negroni is a full stop. I hope you brought your chastity guardian to talk to me!

–What's this about the chastity guardian? - asks Lucia. The lady accompanying Marco also shows interest.

–I'll explain it to you later on. Come and let me introduce you all. Is this your wife, Marco? Hello, I am Leonardo Ruiz, pleased to meet you.

13 Silvia

The afternoon was misty and heavy over Casablanca's international airport. Silvia dozed at intervals in her Royal Air Maroc *business class* seat. It was the first time she was going to set foot on the African continent, but, being a business trip, she wasn't looking forward to it. Jérôme had been to many places in Africa and had given her some basic recommendations about women's status in Islamic countries. She had a mixture of prejudices that ranged from Sherazade to *Not Without My Daughter* to the Afghan burqa. However, she had some Islamic colleagues in the office who had reassured her about this and given her other recommendations that she decided not to share with Jéjé.

–Would you like more *foie gras*, miss? - The colorful and helpful stewardess had been showering her and her cabin mates with attentions throughout the flight.

–No, thank you very much, everything was great.

When she was still a schoolgirl and traveled with her parents by plane, they had once been lucky enough to travel first class, and this flight was reminding her of those times. She wondered why European airlines had lowered the level of service in first-class so drastically. She was crumbling these thoughts as she gazed absorbedly at the fine silverware being used by the stewardess in her trolley when the captain announced that descent was beginning. A few minutes earlier, the sight of the desert out the window reminded her of the beautiful ochres of *The English Patient*. The film's plot had escaped her notice, but its colorfulness had become fixed in her memory.

She would only spend two nights in Casablanca, so she only had a cabin bag and her laptop and did not have to wait. She went straight to the passport queue with his immigration form conveniently filled out. She was surprised to have to show her passport twice, the first time to stamp it and the second time to check that it had been stamped. On the way out, she saw her name on a little blackboard held by a smiling Moorish man dressed all in white. The Moroccan must not yet be twenty years old. As they made their way to the car, she was surprised that Fattah, as he was called, had not offered to carry her suitcase for her.

She wanted to go back to the magazine store to buy some newspapers, but a police officer told her that she could not re-enter the airport through the same door. She had to go through the control gate where the X-ray detector was installed, and then he let her in. The officer had questioned her in Arabic, and it was difficult to make him catch that she did not understand anything.

The palm trees that adorned the airport parking lot and the noticeable temperature difference quickly made her feel the remoteness of her home. She amused herself by gazing out the window at the scenery while replying in monosyllables to Fattah's attempts to engage her in conversation. A few advertisements for real estate developers contrasted with the humble cottages she had seen along the road until she saw a sumptuous villa on the side of the road. Fattah told her that the villa belonged to a major state-owned factory director who was very close to the royal family without being asked.

Arriving in the city, she could see that providence had a hard job dealing with the local driving style. Silvia is Roman and lives in Milan, which is why she had no problem with dizzy driving. She lived with the only adult without a driver's license she had ever met in her life, so the art of driving held no secrets for her. Still, she was intrigued by Fattah's and the other drivers' knack for driving the car at full speed with their eyes fixed anywhere but straight ahead. Jerome, by now, would be squeezing his beret like a lemon.

At the door of the hotel on *Avenue de l'Armée Royale,* she encountered another X-ray control. She was somewhat annoyed, but she was determined not to lose her cool except in case of extreme necessity. The hotel lobby looked like something out of a Tintin comic book. The bellboys were impeccably dressed, and some of the employees and some of the clients wore djellaba. She noticed the unusual number of men with their heads covered. It had always been a pity to her that the hat's custom was dead in Europe, and the Ascot races were a pending account she had with herself. She especially liked the classic Humphrey Bogart hats. She found it completely impossible to get to Casablanca without remembering old *Bogey.* She almost wished her arrival had been in black and white.

She locked herself in her room, dropped her suitcase, took off her shoes, and began to study all the hotel information. There were five restaurants, but she hated eating alone in public places and decided on a *niçoise* salad. She called room service, placed her order, and looked for a music channel on the television. She took off her clothes, makeup, and bathrobe, ready to finish the book she had brought with her after dinner. She didn't have to go over anything for the next day's meeting, and she had always enjoyed the check-in ceremony in hotel rooms. These were unique moments of intimacy with herself. "Alone in Casablanca. I am the Roman Bergman."

Silvia organizes conventions for an American laboratory and travels a lot. Although her activity field is European, she had to come to Casablanca to help in a medical congress's organization to be held in Marrakech at the end of the month. Her boss's intention in sending her was to make clear to the Moroccan distributors the particularities of a couple of doctors who will attend the congress. She would also take advantage of the opportunity to contact the local customs because she did not know the terrain. Silvia had told him that if she wanted to introduce him to Morocco, she would have gladly accepted that the laboratory would subsidize a pleasure trip with her boyfriend to the Atlas, but her arguments did not convince Roberto.

Taller than average, very intelligent, and hard-working, Silvia is one of those professionals who are always good to have around to tame the wild beasts. With angular features and long brown hair, almost always tied back. Light skin with abundant but discreet freckles. She is often commented on for the way she moves. They say she is very feline. Her dance and music studies, which she has been able to combine with a chemistry career, help her give this impression. She adds an unruffled discretion to her occasional verbal acidity and never spares anyone a smile from her thin lips.

Silvia hoped to be able to have children soon. She didn't want to go through the fertility treatments she saw her older sister undergo when diagnosed with ovarian vagus. She also wanted to get married because she understood that she had found her better half and that her better half had found her. Although it had taken her a couple of years to come to that conclusion, she had no doubts about it. Her sister always used to sing the same song to her: "Silvia, choose very well. Look, to take a bastard, you have to be a bitch, and you are a cream pie." She didn't agree on any of the points.

The book she was reading was an essay by Brabaglia on experimental theater. She was in the habit of taking advantage of her trips to read essays and only read novels when in Milan. She thought that this way, she could make the most of the journey without being contaminated by the novels' setting. "Novels are for traveling with the imagination. There's no point in reading them when I'm away from home," she told Jérôme when he asked her about her essayistic hobby. She finished the book, satisfied, turned off the light, and fell asleep. She dreamed of Rick's bar scene.

Major Strasser: What is your nationality?
Rick: I'm drunk.
Captain Renault: What makes Rick a citizen of the world.

When the alarm clock rang, she remembered that the three characters from the bar in her dream were drinking mojito in huge balloon glasses. With the news blaring, she took a brief shower, put on a dark skirt and jacket ensemble, very light makeup, and went downstairs for breakfast. Silvia never wore perfume.

The hotel buffet was ominous. She used to have a salty breakfast and satisfied her appetite with a *harira* soup and a poached egg with *merguez* accompanying a too-watery coffee. She used to drink it *ristretto*, two or three, to start the day with a good caffeine slap. On-time, Fattah was waiting at the door to take her to the laboratory on the city's outskirts. On the way, she was surprised by the national sugar company's huge facilities, which looked more like a military complex than an ordinary company. She was walking with the window open and could hear the muezzins calling for prayer. At that moment, Fattah changed the dial of the car radio to a station broadcasting the Koran reading. Rocked by the litany and in complete silence, she let herself be carried away, immersed in her thoughts.

The morning was relatively quiet. She did not understand why everyone insisted on speaking Arabic when they perfectly knew that she could only communicate in French. However, during the meeting, she managed to compromise with this attitude, which she found surreal. The boss was translating for her, but it was clear that everyone in the room was bilingual. Once the meeting was over, and they were all confident, they all switched to French to address her. They headed down the street to a van that would take them to lunch. She could not help but comment on her surprise to Rachida, director of pharmacy sales and the only other woman attending the meeting.

–It's because of the hierarchy, and so you don't get scared of our ways. It's part of the African charm. You'll understand, - she explained while removing her headscarf, and they settled into their seats.

From that angle, she understood it better. Indeed the treatment of boss to subordinate was more aggressive than she was used to. Rachida herself had inadvertently demonstrated this to her by berating Fattah for his poor parking skills. He sensed that Rachida was obliged to apply herself more fervently because of her status as a manager in an eminently male environment. She later told him that she was neither married nor considering it because she refused to take an irreversible break in her career.

They were all taken to a charming fish restaurant in the port of Mohammedia, which she forgot to take the card but liked. Jéjé always insisted on taking the card of every place she went to. The name was no mystery to remember: *Restaurant du Port*. Silvia ordered a sea bass couscous on Rachida's recommendation, and the atmosphere of the meal was suitably convivial.

–So, Miss Casonato, won't you stay with us for a few more days? Your presence is a freshwater pitcher for my eyes - commented the general manager at dessert. The others did not even flinch - If you stretch the weekend, I can show you Marrakech myself.

–No, thank you very much. I assure you that I would love to, I have to make my wedding preparations. My dress is designed by a Catalan who only comes to Milan once a year, and on Saturday, I have the whole day to myself. I am very grateful to you - she gives him a flirtatious wink in revenge for his audacity. Of course, there was no wedding and no Catalan.

–It's a shame. I hope it won't stop you from showing me around your town when I'm passing through. Well, I have to leave you. Rachida will take you to see a couple of clients in the afternoon - Mr. Bounana got up from his seat in a gentle attitude and kissed her hand - Don't forget to come back to see us if you have the chance. My offer will still stand. Have a good trip.

–*Shukran jazilan*, Mr. Bounana. I will not fail to keep it in mind - "Man has no shame" she said to herself while raising her best smile.

It wasn't that Silvia wasn't used to big game hunting. In fact, in Italy, it is a national sport. The insinuation just threw her off in front of everyone at a work meeting. When they were returning to the van, she asked Rachida about the incident.

–Hey, Rachida. Is Bounana like that with all women? I'm a little bit taken aback by her invitation.

–Oh, don't worry. It's only like that with the exotic ones. He is Mauritanian and has four wives. The youngest is twenty years old.

–Twenty years the younger? - She made an astonished face and put her hand to her heart. Well, that's part of the African charm, I guess.

–Yes, as far as we know, he had a lot of trouble getting his first wife to agree to the marriage. Without her consent, they could not have married. Now she treats her like another daughter. Don't make that face, girl. You people are sequential polygamists with your divorces. Here we women exercise our authority in different ways, that's all.

Silvia didn't know if "exotic" was a compliment disguised as a jab or a jab disguised as a compliment, but she felt both sensations. The van dropped them off at the offices, and they both left in Rachida's car to visit some pharmacies in the city.

She was very interested in the visits. They were treated very well in all the pharmacies. Seeing green crescents at pharmacies instead of her usual crosses made her feel far away from everything. They visited the old Medina and bought quite a few silver beads, including a Fatima hand for her sister and some slippers for her man. By now, they were both tuned in and laughing at anything. Passing in front of a terrace where only men had tea, they threw a few compliments at them. Rachida well-instructed her not to turn around under any circumstances, but she found them witty.

They decided to stop by the women's *hammam* before dinner. While they both received their massages on two stone benches in a room completely lined with pink marble, some women, in turn, went in and out to access a doorway in the room. They came out visibly relaxed.

The *gommage* with a special glove and hot water gushing from the fountain seemed like fifth heaven to her.

–Rachida. What's behind that door?

–Ah! If you cross that gate, you will never be the same person. It's part of the African charm - she smiled.

–Silvia crossed the gate without hesitation. She had not traveled so far to miss the African charm.

The next morning, she got up early so as not to miss her plane. They had dined at La Mer on delicious fish after the hammam and had some juices at Rick's Café. It had nothing to do with its Brussels counterpart. It was a more faithful reproduction of the one in the movie, which had been filmed entirely in Hollywood studios. *Bogey* never set foot in Casablanca. She called Jéjé before takeoff and was incredibly affectionate with him.

-Chérie -Have you had such a hard time? You're never this cuddly on the phone.

–I don't know, my love. Come and pick me up at the airport, come on. I love you very much.

She hung up and curled up on the comfortable leather seat. Her cheeks were still flushed, and her face was still flushed with joy. She dreamed the entire flight of African enchantment. Sam played the piano with his eyes in her dream while holding his hands behind his back.

    Yvonne: Where were you last night?
Rick: Last night? I have no idea.
Yvonne: And what are you doing tonight?
Rick: I don't plan that far in advance.

14 Crescent Quarter

Marco and his wife, Maria, initially only came to say hello to some acquaintances and then quickly come back home. That's what they told us, but it seems that they are losing respect for their schedule. Especially Marco, who seems to be in his element, chatting with all of us and greeting people left and right.

The musical proposal of the night is original. It is a rock and roll band with two DJs integrated as if they were two more instrumentalists. One of the DJs is in the booth behind the band. The other one is installed on one of the balconies under the gallery's dome, displays on the screens. Next to the latter are a pair of saxophonists and a trumpet. In addition to the classic instruments since John and Paul put on the tie, the band has a tribal percussion group and three female voices backing vocals.

According to the program, they only play covers, planned in an ascending line from the 70's to the 10's. At first glance, the result is very encouraging: all the musicians are experts at what they do, and they cram the classics with their improvisations. The whole party is dancing, and we are no exception. The waiters have stopped distributing Asti and now fall in waves. Some go in groups of three with trolleys spreading cocktails and mixed drinks to the attendees, and others carry bowls of ice bristling with skewers of fresh fruit, followed closely by trays of three melted chocolates for the fruit.

We don't get to the point where we have to squeeze, and there is room to dance comfortably—Lucia rocks and rolls with the grace of a panther. There is a lot of rock tradition in France, and dancing is somewhat different from the American way. When the others are refilling drinks, we decide to take the plunge and seek out the restrooms.

We walk hand in hand like two schoolboys through the crowd. As we leave the central hall, we tell each other our impressions.

–You dance very well, Lucia. And you still haven't dropped your new dress, which, by the way, fits you very well.

–Thank you, you little shrink. You're not bad yourself. Hey, have you seen what a good couple the duke and the Brazilian girl make? They look great together. They look like they've just stepped out of a Cinderella story.

I don't know what cable crosses my mind at that moment. I don't know if it's the bath with Sandra, the waltz, or the Asti. I don't know if it's Lucia's fresh cheek or what. The fact is that I stop, immerse myself in her deep gaze for an eternal instant, grab her by the waist, and we give each other a deep kiss during which neither of us looks away from the other's eyes.

Lucia tastes like mango with strawberry. I must have a pleasing aroma of sparkling wine. What did Richard Gere say? No, it's not the taste. It's the sum of factors. La Scala will never again be what it was for any of us gathered there celebrating the newspaper's anniversary.

My mind is miles away when, suddenly, it is forced back. Lucia, somewhat disturbed, puts an end to the magic of the kiss by separating abruptly.

–It's not right, I can't, I don't know if I want to. I don't know what I was thinking - her colors rise, she turns around and walks away among the dancers towards the restroom. I stand there, stunned.

–Lucia...

While I try to understand what could be wrong with a kiss and I start to blame myself for my impulsiveness, I follow the path where Lucia has gone, and I cross paths with Silvia and Jéjé.

–Leonardo! *Mon petit père*! You look like you're hallucinating. Are you having a good time?

–Hi Leo, long time no see, - says Silvia. I give her two kisses and try to pull myself together as best I can.

–My favorite couple! Congratulations to both of you. It's a non-stop party. Jéjé, I feel deeply betrayed.

–Betrayed? That's a good one, Silvia. He brings me three more guests to the party. I put them all in the VIP area and welcomes us like this. You're not Spanish, are you? Hahaha! - Finally, I hear the ferret and the turkey again, our Jéjé is back.

–Of course, you're Belgian! Don't pay any attention to him, Silvia. We Spaniards, first and foremost, are gentlemen, and this scoundrel hasn't had the courtesy to offer me even a job as an errand boy in this marvelous place. We met last month, you animal!

–I think he's right, *mon chou*, - Silvia replied. - Since you've been through everything together what you went through in Bonn, it wouldn't have hurt to bring Leo in as a shoeshine boy. His shoes have always been impeccable. I think that all of Jéjé's quirks come from your living together.

—Very funny about the shoeshine boy, Roman babe. I see that living with this jerk hasn't affected you at all yet. You two look great. I would have even come as a shoeshine boy and for free. Are you staying here, or are you still organizing, Jéjé? You look like an air traffic controller with your headphones.

—I'm free now, but I'm keeping an eye on the operation for what might happen - he takes off his earpiece and puts it to my ear. - Look, you ruffian. This will be of interest to you for your social experiments. Don't say anything. The mic is online.

As I put it on, I feel a little dizzy at first. The headset must be made of some special latex, and it clings to the ear like a suction cup, covering it completely. The isolation is almost absolute, so that through the right ear, I hear something similar to a mixture of a NASA checkpoint with the latest sci-fi blockbuster, while with the left ear, I hear the music and our conversation. It takes me some time to adjust, but it's incredible. In my right ear, I hear almost no music from the party, only robotic voices.

—Area 3 covered. Three cup carts to area two. Free area two?

—Alpha one to control. We immediately cover area two.

–Beta three to control. Ten percent ice.

–Alpha four to Beta three. Copy that.

–Door two to Control. Two drunks to sickbay. Class C guests.

–Control to all. Nursing cases have no class distinction.

I am shocked. He must have noticed because Jéjé explains it to me right away.

–Impressive, isn't it? It's a new software-controlled system that connects to the stereo and performs room sound mixer damping on each earphone in real-time. Don't ask me how they do it, but you already see the result. Or rather, listening.

No sooner has she finished the sentence, I feel a powerful pull on the other ear that makes the microphone fall inside the glass I was sipping and then fall to the floor. Lucia, without letting go of my ear, kisses me again, this time without remorse. The underwater microphone is causing a little auditory chaos in all the system users, including myself until I notice how Jéjé removes it from my ear.

–Hahahaha! Come, Silvia. I have to change my earphones. Now we'll see Leo, who seems to be enjoying the party. I hope he introduces us to his friend.

–So long, Leo. Don't leave without having a drink with us.

I say goodbye without looking with a wave of my hand. It's hard for me to think. Lucia is destroying my ear, and I don't want to ruin this kiss. We both approach some awkwardness to find some solace in one of the boxes on the upper floor. I have to go to the bathroom, but I'm holding on like a Don Quixote. I'm not going to be left without my Dulcinea again.

After a long time of kisses and caresses on a comfortable sofa on the second floor, the band starts playing *Azzurro,* and the whole audience joins in loudly. We can't get away from the catchy chorus either. I see Pietro from above. Decidedly practical in his red tuxedo. When dancing while playing the guitar in the air, he looks even more like his impersonation. He's talking to Jéjé and Sandra to Silvia. They have probably introduced themselves. I don't see Marco and his wife.

–Lucia, you're wonderful. But you've been told that a hundred times already. Would you like another drink? If you don't run away from me, I'll get it for you.

–You just want to go to the toilet, you little shrink. Your legs have been shaking for a while now.

–My legs have nothing to do with that. It's the terror of your big eyes - I caress her face.

–You talk too much, you little shrink. But you're a good kisser - she pulls my hand away, and we kiss again. - Come on, let's go downstairs. I can't wait to dance. Go to the bathroom, you liar.

–Promise you won't run away like before. I wouldn't forgive myself.

–Yes, a pumpkin awaits me at the Duomo. Come on, you donkey!

Lucia has taken a liking to pull my ears. It hurts, but it binds. Along the way, I get a few tugs before we separate to make my long-delayed visit. There's a queue for the toilets, and people enter in pairs, the usual. The lounge music booms on mute in the bathroom to the rhythm of the cheerful and vibrant self-medication advocates' noses. I remember my younger years with a certain nostalgia every time I witness a similar scene, and they are not few. I believe that the double standard is of little use in avoiding collapses in psychiatric care centers, but concerning drugs, I still think that all that money ends up in Swiss accounts would be much better spent on schools, hospitals and roads.

I arrive where the others are dancing and chatting animatedly. The volume makes it possible to do both, as long as you are within talking distance. When, once again, the sexes' war has put the boys with the boys and the girls with the girls, we commend Jéjé for his carefully staged performance. They are dancing to *Billie Jean*.

–It's unique what you have done. I'm very grateful to Sandra and Leonardo for having me come here. I've seen some of your people with circumspect faces as the Nomad Party tragicomedy unfolded.

–Not at all, Pietro, - answered Jérôme. - As they say, envy is the way imbeciles admire. We are delighted with the result, and I agree with you that I could consider giving it something more than poetry if the idea works.

–What has me in awe is the budget you have invested in making this whole set-up. I'll be indiscreet. How much did the joke cost you?

–That's classified, as you can guess, *mon petit père*. Anyway, you know me, much of the expense is covered by advertising. The most aberrant thing has been the Colombian singer's cache, but I insisted on having her with us at any cost. She is capable of bringing down a stadium with a hip strike. If she hadn't left, I'd introduce her to you. She's a more than bearable diva. I like the orchestra. I was inspired by a biweekly party in Paris, close to where we went to that *house* session. Do you remember, Leo?

–I remember, yes. It was terrific that night. And I see that Martine got what you wanted very well. That also had a significant effect.

–What do you mean? - asks Pietro.

–It refers to the intro mix with the classical orchestra. Martine is a friend of ours. She and her husband could not come because Philippe's mother is undergoing chemotherapy. I spoke with her this afternoon, and she told me that the results are optimistic.

–Good for Philou's mother! Wear whatever you want, but I want a copy of that stuff. I can think of a couple of ideas to play with it.

–If it's possible, I'm interested too. Let me take this opportunity to give you my card. Ah! Don't forget to check our catalog. I'm sure you'll find something.

–Thank you, Pietro. I'll email you a copy, don't worry. I'll have to reduce it because it's a master, and it comes in a huge file. It arrived just this morning. It would have been a pity not to have it, just like the theater. I suggest we go to the gallery. Soon the tone of the night will change, and I think you will like it.

As we cross the bridge over the plaza, a man stops to greet Silvia. He looks quite cheerful. The truth is that we're all already sucked like custard apples, but, as in all black-tie celebrations, restraint is kept a little longer, and few men have yet let go of their jackets.

–Congratulations to both of you! I just got back from the congress in Marrakech, and I heard about your wedding. I was just surprised not to have received the invitation. - Jéjé is completely livid and, without saying a word, waits for Silvia's answer.

–Hahaha! Bounana told you that, didn't he? No, there is no wedding. It was an excuse I made up to get out of the way. Bounana is a bit of a predator.

–Oh, well. Well, that's a pity. Let's see when the two of you settle down because this woman is in great demand - she elbows Jéjé in the gut and gives Silvia a wink - Well, excuse me, but I can't let my little group run away. I've left my contact lenses behind, and I can't see anyone more than five meters away. See you on Monday. Great party!

As Silvia's companion leaves for the theater, she affectionately reprimands Jéjé.

–Of course, I have a showroom groom! Can you make that face when you hear the word "wedding"? I'm losing hope in you.

–No, Silvia, you don't have a boyfriend, I'm just your partner - Silvia squeezes her purse as if she was going to throw it in his face - I made the face I did because I was looking for the ideal moment, and that moment has just found me. Please accept this ring, and then we'll be engaged - Will you marry me?

Saying this, Jérôme takes out of his jacket pocket a small box with an engagement ring set with sapphire and diamond baguettes forming a rune. Silvia's face is a poem. Under the watchful eye of my stone namesake, between La Scala and the Vittorio Emanuele gallery, Silvia and Jérôme seal their engagement with a fierce kiss. We decide to discreetly outshine each other and let them enjoy their unique moment.

No matter how many times we see the same scene in movies, theaters, or real life. No matter how armored one is, as in my case, because I had my ring moment, I will have it again when the time comes. The part of our brain dealing with feelings is a voracious devourer of grandiloquent gestures. One only has to attend any ceremony, whatever its nature, to see how fond we humans are of satisfying this expectation. Similarly, it is notorious how these special moments in our lives are engraved in our subconscious and often help us overcome other painful ones. Jérôme and Silvia hold all the cards for a fruitful and lasting relationship.

We decided to pay homage to the white bull again to wish the future spouses luck.

–At the heel, everyone has to say a wish out loud, - says Sandra, as she is busy squeezing the bull's balls with her pink Mascaró. I ask for four children - Pietro catches her on the fly and makes his wish.

–I also ask for four children! We already have something in common, Miss Gomes. Do you know how children are made?

–I'll give you lessons whenever you want, *duquezinho*. But don't count on me for the practical part as long as you don't become an orphan. Your mother has a very bad reputation.

–That's Lucia's stuff. Mom is very easy to get along with, I'll introduce you to her.

–I'm asking for a proposal like Silvia's. How nice it was! What are you asking for, you little shrink?

–I ask that this poor animal does not come to populate our nightmares because of the cruelty and recidivism with which we are treating it. What more can I wish for if the queen of the party has become attached to my ears? - Lucia returns the compliment with a good tug.

15 Full Moon

We're back to the lychee martini bar. The four of us are having an excellent time toasting and making jokes, and the band leaves while a devilish organ starts to play over the speakers. As the volume rises, all the lights go out, and we see how huge black curtains with abstract motifs in light strokes are covering all the facades. Some blacklight LEDs are turned on, and I look again at Sandra's teeth' whiteness, which have become the center of her face. The gallery gets filled with cold smoke. Waiters dressed as skeletons and very well characterized start to come out. They are carrying trays full of wireless studio headphones that they are handing out to the audience and are being followed by jugglers with torches. The spectacle is overwhelming. A shallow drum begins to play slowly and gradually imposes its presence while an announcer introduces the session. Through the screens, a single spotlight illuminates the booth inside the theater.

"Ladies and gentlemen, the hour of darkness has come. The time has come to leave our mark on this century-old floor. The gallery is purgatory, and the theater is hell, but with the props you are being given, you will be able to feel the flame while in purgatory. Take care of your souls and welcome with a round of applause for..... DJ Chastity!"

Lucia jumps.

–DJ Chastity! That's Chloé! She's here to DJ!

We look at the screens and see Chloé come out under the spotlight with a head covering and a crimson robe while the drum is roaring in a bestial way. We can barely hear the applause from the audience. Chloé removes her bonnet, puts on large helmets, and settles into the controls of the booth. She starts strong and mournful, linking the drum with the radio tune of "La noche escabrosa" in a satanic mix when the skulls are still walking insolently along the avenue. The nun is good. Everybody dances and we are no exception.

A skeleton hands us our headphones, and, like the rest, we put them around our necks while we continue dancing. Actors on stilts move through the crowd, and on the screens, we see a percussion group accompanying Chloé on stage. All righteousness left is now lost. Men leave their jackets, and bow ties in the closets, and women make ingenious and suggestive figures with their dresses. DJ Chastity is consecrating the *Giornale del Mondo*! Lucia tells me that she does it as a *hobby* with great success. She does one session a month in different European cities. I can barely fill the dots with our brief chat at the Duomo a few hours earlier.

After half an hour of high vibes, the music drops from the speakers in the gallery, linking smoothly with *chill-out* music, which comes commanded from the balcony set. Through the headphones, you can still hear the frantic deep house session of La Scala, which continues to be seen on the screens mixed with aerial views of the party and some interviews from when we were still dressed up. The mix is hilarious. The part under the gallery's dome keeps the rhythm with all the dancers wearing helmets, and the sofas regain the relaxed tone with soft glimpses of jazz, bossa, and ethnic music. We decide to take a break with another round of martinis in a lounge before heading back to La Scala. I receive an SMS "How do you like the gathering, *mon petit père?*"

We meet Jéjé at the Scala dance floor. When we get there, Silvia and Jéjé are dancing animatedly with the basketball player, named Ronald. We all start dancing with them furiously. Lucia, Silvia, and Sandra move like jungle folk in some initiation ceremony. The drums make the room shake. Colored lights invade my head. We laugh, we jump, we play, we shout! Pump it up, Chloé!!!!

CHRONOSOPHY OF THE FOX AND THE RAVEN

Quae se laudari gaudent verbis subdolis,
serae dant poenas turpi paenitentia.
Cum de fenestra corvus raptum caseum
comesse vellet, celsa residens arbore,
vulpes invidit, deinde sic coepit loqui:
'O qui tuarum, corve, pinnarum est nitor!
Quantum decoris corpore et vultu geris!
Si vocem haberes, nulla prior ales foret'.
At ille, dum etiam vocem vult ostendere,
lato ore emisit caseum; quem celeriter
dolosa vulpes avidis rapuit dentibus.
Tum demum ingemuit corvi deceptus stupor.

—I'm sick of you always stealing the scene from me, fox! Next time you climb the tree to sing, and I'll take the cheese.

—*It's always the same old song, crow. The fable is like that. It's like that, and that's it. Besides, you tell me, how long has it been since we performed it in Latin?*

—*Well, you're damn right, fox. At least five hundred cycles. Whose is this one?*

—*It's always the same, crow. It doesn't matter if they call him Aesop, Phaedrus, Lafontaine, Samaniego. It's always the same. They are archetypes. Have you forgotten the day you were hired? It was very clear.*

—*Yes, I remember, yes. It would have been better for me to do like my cousin, the one who accompanies the witch. He doesn't go through the hardships I do, and you always eat the cheese in one bite! Let's see if someday you'll leave me a little piece, for the sake of fellowship and all that.*

—*Well, if you knew how I always feel like eating it with some grapes I've seen.... You know, "grapes with cheese, they taste like a kiss." No chance, every time I see the grapes to bring them here, they're green!*

—*You're diverting the conversation, fox. Next time, instead of singing, I'll bite and what's left over is for you.*

—*You can't do that. You'll ruin the archetype! We're out of a job! Besides, you couldn't even if you wanted to. Archetypes are eternal and immutable. The boss said so.*

—*Did he say that? I don't remember ever hearing him say that. Let's take off our make-up and then go home. There are no more sessions today. I'll wait for you on the way out.*

—*It's okay, it's okay.*

They went into their dressing rooms to get dressed. The fox had a wonderful green satin dress, and the raven ran into his impeccable morning coat. They had been married since the raven was hired for the fable because his predecessor could no longer sing due to pharyngitis that turned out to be chronic.

Returning home in the theater carriage, they resumed their discussion.

—What I don't understand is why we have to act naked. Look at the dress the eagle has given me to beg for pardon.

—I don't think it's fair that you still see your ex. That eagle has a lot of feathers to make you gifts, I guess. We know each other well among birds. He's looking for something.

—Don't talk nonsense, you fool. If I married you, it's because I love you, isn't it? Whoever cheats, what he is showing is how poorly he chose his partner. Come on, show me that little golden beak.

—Well, I know what I'm saying. Don't give me this or that. I prefer it when you play with the statue or the frog. I'm more comfortable with them.

—What about my virtual reality goggles? I'm going to spend the whole night wandering around today.

—Yes, they were brought in this morning.

—Oh well, you can always set them up, and I'll wear yours. Yesterday I wanted to go for a walk in Vietnam. There was a festival.

—It's as good as it gets with delivery. I'm sorry. I'm sorry.

—It's okay, as long as they're here today. You know how it is. Every human who sees the archetype we represent is available on the console to enter their dreams or trance states. Dreams are very boring, but in trances you can see the world of humans and, when you're lucky, hilarious things happen to you.

—It is true that there are many more sleepers to choose from than trances. And also that, in dreams, it's always more of the same. Let's see what's playing today.

Arrived home, the crow put on his slippers, and the fox went straight to the kitchen to prepare dinner. She didn't think much about it. A couple of omelets and some custard for dessert, two glasses of white wine they bought in the king's castle, and straight to the console.

—Omelette again, fox? We could vary a little, my love.

—Tomorrow, you'll make dinner. The guy must complain... Turn on the console, come on. Let's choose something fun.

—It's always omelet, and omelet again. Wasn't there a little cheese?

—It says so in the contract, weirdo. As long as you work with that fable, cheese is forbidden. I'm deprived of more things. I do a lot of plays. In the end, you only work in three. I'm going to ask for a leave to get my fill of grapes once and for all.

—Let's see what my "habitués" are doing. Look, look, with this girl I saw again "Casablanca" recently, semi-colored. She's at a party in Milan, and there are a lot of them. We're going to be able to walk everywhere.

–*Come on, select that one. I haven't seen Milan for a long time.*

They both lay down on the sofa and put on their glasses. They strolled around La Scala and the Vittorio Emanuele under Chloé's baton and had a great time. On a couple of occasions, they met on the runway and greeted each other while making faces. The fox took part in a couple of debates on the segregation of Northern Italy, and, sick of it, she spent the rest of the time on the dance floor.

The crow spent most of his time between the gallery and the bathroom. He met the frog and the monkey, and they both kept flirting with the frog, going back and forth between the clusters of guests who were all having very original and racy conversations.

–*Puff, what a party! You're having fun, little crow?*

–*Ah! Yes, indeed. Do you want to turn off the console now?*

–*My side, yes, I haven't stopped dancing. Let's go to bed.*

–*What I like the most is when you're talking to someone who hasn't seen the fable. It's like talking to the wall. It's fun! I've seen the monkey and the frog. Have you crossed paths with anyone?*

–*Besides you, I've only seen Alice's cat, but he's always at every party. I don't know how she does it. Some hack, I'm sure.*

–*Well, I'm picking this up.*

—As they were picking up, the beep-beep of the fox's pager in her purse sounded. She read the message and was outraged.

"The fox and the eagle - Extraordinary session in half an hour - Come urgently".

—Can't you just have a normal day? I'm going to ask for that leave right now. I'm going to ask for it! This is abuse!

—I see you are quite upset. It had to be the eagle, right? Do you want to tell me something, fox?

—Look, I don't have time for your bullshit. I'm flying. It's in half an hour.

The fox went up to the dressing room and came down with stunning looks. She was wearing the same dress. The one the eagle had given to her.

—You are a bit daring. Couldn't you at least wear another dress?

—Aaargh! I'm sick of you all! I dumped that one because he was also hopelessly jealous. Come and see the show with me if you want, but you've been warned, either you show a little more confidence, or you're going to go to the friendzone with the other "feathered" one. The statue has already got its eye on me, by God!

—The fox left with a huge slamming of the door. The crow gave a deep sigh and started to review the tapes where he had recorded "Casablanca". He wondered whether to call the frog, or sneak into the theater to try to catch his wife in the act.

-She's a bitch, the fox! - He thought with a frown as he threw himself back on the couch.

The raven, ashamed and confused,
Sweared, but a little late, that he would never be
caught again.

225

16 Waning Quarter

Lucia has paid a visit to Chloé in the cabin and announced that she was close to finishing. We decide to rest a little and go back to the sofa area. Sandra and Pietro are still dancing. Jérôme and Silvia are ecstatic. Now the waiters are distributing chocolates and sweets. You have to fetch the glasses from the bar. The truth is that we're all severely hurt. All of us and everyone around us. Ronald proposes a game. You have to join phrases that link with each other, as the chained words but with sayings. He begins.

—If you know who said the phrase, don't forget to quote it. The first one, I don't remember who said it. Here goes: "In the beginning was the verb."

–In the end, the "bla-bla-bla-bla" is by an author, I swear, but I can't remember who, either, - says Silvia, and we all laugh.

–"Life is a lottery. Even if you win, in the end you lose your life", this is from a French song - returns Jéjé.

–"We don't need the lottery. We have each other," Lucia says, scratching my knee. I like her more and more.

–"A DJ only lives from others. He plays other people's music to make other people dance" by Beigbeder. Ronald's little game is fine, but I think I've had a little too much to drink - I add.

–"Today, I'm going to pause for a thousand bars," is another song - says Silvia.

–Hey! That's got nothing to do with it, *amour*. You can't.

–I can't? Look how I'm doing it! I love the game, but I'm going to the bathroom to pout in front of the mirror. Are you coming, Lucia?

The two of them leave. The three of us remain in animated conversation.

–Wow, Ronald. You're the first American I've met who likes charades. I quite enjoyed your talk earlier, especially when you developed the need for contenders in sports. It is a curious counterpoint to the bipartisanship that Jéjé deplores.

–Don't believe any of the clichés that circulate about the culture of these people, Leo. They own the media, and we have the image of America they want us to have - Jéjé takes out a wet wipe and rubs it on his face -. I've met a lot of neurons over there and a lot of solidarity. Ben Franklin was by no means an isolated case, *mon petit père.*

–Hahaha! You're both very funny, *pals.* Especially you, Jérôme. Everyone around here indeed thinks we're a pitiful country of alienated people, full of junk food and little flags in the windows who swallow everything that comes on CNN. The Simpsons keep helping us give that image. How many blacks are there in the front line of European sport who have scientific studies and have gone through the world's second most demanding army? I know a few in my homeland. It's a good thing you think we're dumb. We still love your decadent way of doing and seeing things.

–Our decadent way of doing things also has a lot to do with traditions, - I infer. - With traditions and with questioning. I still remember that phrase that was circulated when the towers came down. Why do they hate us? Have you found out? Do you know if it is you they hate?

–Look. Our culture is all about empathy. About empathy and about the most practical way of doing things. On a technological level, we always build from scratch every time. You guys always add stones to the same castle. I'm not arguing which is better or worse, but the fact is that dynamism is our flag, pals. Why do they hate us? The question comes from the deepest part of our hearts. We are sincere even when we lye! You think we want to impose our democracy and follow the *pax americana*. JFK said it, that's not what we want. We want a peaceful world because every time we are on our own, it is the rest of the world that comes to us asking us to solve their problems.

–That could have been so in the world wars, *mon petit père*. If I remember correctly, Saddam's greatest sin was that he wanted to start selling oil in Euros, and that did not suit your hegemony at all.

–Yes, there is a battle for energy. Of course, there is. Yes, we alternate hard-handed governments with soft-handed governments, too, pal. Yes, we manage a bunch of radicals of all stripes. But our American dream that you despise so much is what has put us where we are. Do you think we should think about changing our dream because it is outside your standards? I'm sticking to the practical: show us what you do best, we will have no problem adapting. Adapting is what we do best. The job is yours, not ours. I go back to the Simpsons. They help us laugh at ourselves.

–We don't need the Simpsons - I interrupt - We have enough with yours and our TV trash.

What we want is for you to keep us in mind and not forget where you come from. Weak memory causes the repetition of mistakes.

–And we are suspicious of that sincerity you mention, - says Jéjé. - It is very nice to hear "Yes, we can" and it is also true that we reply "Yes, you should". But your governments are voracious, and your dark side often leaves ours with a bib, if I may say so.

–Hahaha! It's okay, pals. We're not going to solve the fifth cold war today. While you're looking for our faults, we're too busy looking ahead. Waiter! Would you bring me another orange juice?

The waiter looks questioningly at Jéjé, who nods. The girls return from the bathroom and bring with them Chloé, who has taken off her tunic and is the only one in the whole party wearing jeans. The three of them are laughing their heads off.

–Hey guys, look who we ran into! She was quarreling on the runway with a security guard who relieved her of her joint. They almost didn't take it off his belt!

–I've been harassed! Pietro pulls me out of bed because I wasn't on time to DJ your session, and I have to endure censorship when I start dancing for a while. Hi, you must be Jérôme. I'm a friend of Carlo's and, as you know, your spare DJ today. Luckily he's already arrived, and I've left him the set. You must be paying him very well because apart from seeing you all so happy, the check he gave me is the only thing that made me smile tonight.

–Yes, I'm Jérôme, and I thank you a lot for the effort and the quality! You mix very well. I didn't know at all that you had anything to do with each other. You know Silvia. This is Ronald, a one-night stand collaborator who comes from across the pond and gives us all chins.

–Hello, Ronald. Don't get up. I don't want to wake up with a stiff neck. With me, it's three kisses. Where I was born, it would be two and in the North of France four, but I have become accustomed to Provence because of an old story. Hi Leo! I have already been told that they will put your name on the white list in Palermo. Be careful with the *famiglia*. You know how it is. Hihi! No news about the duke and the Brazilian?

–Very ingenious, Joan of Arc. What a pity that the bouncer didn't frisk you to remove your stuff. We haven't seen the couple since we left La Scala.

–Sit down here with me, - Ronald says to Chloé. - I've never been to France, and I'd like you to instruct me. I'm going to be in Paris next week.

Chloé settles in, and the two of them start talking and smoking. Jéjé proposes to Lucia and me to accompany them to an appointment they have with Tavola. He has been warned with a laser pointer from the gallery booth. So the four of us go. The meeting is in a hotel suite, so we leave the party to access the reception through the back street, and we get at a somewhat nondescript anteroom where Giorgio is waiting for us. He welcomes us with a pleasant gesture and a wide smile.

–It's a pleasure, young people. Jérôme's friends are also my friends. As a promise is a promise, Jéjé, I have brought with me Chinamano from Zimbabwe. Chinamano is the shaman of his tribe, and once a year, he is received by several heads of state.

–Heads of state? - I ask, - But nobody believes in anything today.

–Well, you might be surprised to know that the first people Chinamano started visiting are the presidents of Cuba and Venezuela. I met him while attending a refugee camp, and he is an exceptional old man. Will the four of you go in? The room is ready.

The proposal catches Lucia, Sonia, and me by surprise. Jéjé smiles looking at our faces. The girls crack up. Lucia answers first.

–I don't like these things. Where I come from, we have enough with the harsh reality. I'm not going.

–I don't dare either, - says Silvia. But don't keep yourself from asking about our future, *mon petit papa*. Because you already had this one ready, you bastard. Your eyes are shining.

–Well, - says Tavola, - all that remains is to find out how macho the males are.

Jérôme looks ready and eager. I feel caught between a rock and a hard place, and I have no choice but to nod. I don't find it very funny because I make my living from psychology, and I have studied shamanism very well. The shaman is a catalyst. He is the priest, the magician, the druid, the doctor, the wisest of madmen, and the maddest of wise men. He is hardly among us because his mind is constantly riding on the back of the Leviathan. I read Castaneda's writings long ago and learned a lot from Don Juan. I also experimented with psychedelic drugs for study purposes and discovered corners of my psyche that, in some cases, I didn't quite like. Now then, in the context of the party, as high as I am, and if the Don Juan of Tavola has confronted the incombustible Galician of Sierra Maestra, I can expect anything. I reluctantly step forward in approval, and Tavola ushers us into the room. I kiss Lucia goodbye like a condemned man on death row. Her hands are cold.

The room is in semi-darkness. A few bowls of oil with wicks make the flames dance and show our shadows on the walls. Music from the gallery can still be heard, and the bass has much more presence, contributing to the solemn atmosphere of the improvised cavern that Tavola has organized. There is also a strong smell of burning laurel. Laurel was the drug of choice for the murderous bacchantes in ancient Greek times because of its high cyanide content. Of course, to get any effect on the lentils, you would have to use a whole plant. Jérôme, in Bonn, had given me some lessons in culinary alchemy. From his recipes, I still make the pasta with zucchini sauce: garlic and zucchini are grated and divided by three; in a base of olive oil, the first third is roasted, the second is made to lose water, and the third is left almost raw, a drop of white wine, coarsely ground black pepper and a handful of cheese at the end. In this way, the papillae make the three cooking processes' complete journey, masterful and straightforward.

Chinamano is waiting for us, squatting in front of a large metal plate placed on stones where a tiny bonfire is burning where he is throwing the laurel leaves. He has a bone mortar between his legs and is surrounded by a pile of small colored pots that he is using to prepare his strange mixture. The man is skeletal. He looks as if he has just come out of Dachau. His skin is bluish-black, and he has a very curly, very ragged gray beard. His head is wrapped in a white cloth, and a kind of thread blanket is wrapped around his body in complicated knots. He is humming a soft melody in a heavy rhythm that he accompanies with his head. When he sees us enter, he welcomes Tavola with a distracted smile, showing us his only tooth, immense and the color of elephants' tusks. After this fleeting gesture, he resumes his chant, as if Jéjé and I were not present. In front of him and on the other side of the bonfire are a few piles of thin hemp ropes. Tavola asks us to make ourselves comfortable near the ropes and, without asking for approval, begins to tie our wrists behind our backs. I look at Jéjé anxiously, and he answers me with an accomplice smile and a mischievous look. Tavola also ties our ankles.

Chinamano speaks only Sindebele. Tavola sits next to him and translates for us. We are both tied up like sausages, sitting and looking at each other face to face. I feel ridiculous and a little humiliated, but let's see how far the comedy goes. Chinamano is giving instructions while pronouncing incantations. He paints our faces with parsimony. Jérôme is quite frightened, so I understand that I must be no less.

–Tonight - translates Tavola - you are going to meet the dark king. Nothing bad will happen to you. Stick out your tongue - Chinamano paints our tongue with a brush. He is using the mortar mixture as the only ingredient -. Papa China's preparation will remove from your spirit any trace of goodness you may harbor. Its effect will last a few minutes, then we will untie you, and you will write in those notebooks what you remember. You will have to keep those writings with you until life teaches you what is due to you. You may not show them to anyone or discuss your experience except amongst yourselves. Each visit by the dark king is unique. Do not forget, nothing bad will happen to you.

—Guelele lele lele lele lele lele lele lele leeeeeeeeeeeee - Chinamano starts repeating - Guelele lele lele lele lele lele lele leeeeeeeeeeee!

The sorcerer leaves a huge knife on the ground at the same distance from both of them. The taste of his concoction is repulsive, spicy, and bitter. I feel as if my cerebellum is beginning to pulsate.

—You must stare at the knife. Your head will hurt. The pain is induced. It is false. Don't stop staring at the knife. Nothing bad will happen to you.

—Guelele lele lele lele lele lele lele leeeeeeeeeeee!

I'm seriously regretting having let myself be fooled into this. It's too late now. My head hurts. It is a pain that grows, that invades. Jérôme and I start screaming without taking our eyes off the knife. We both lose our balance and start crawling on the ground like worms without taking our eyes off the knife. I scream at the top of my lungs. I see Jerome screaming. I force myself to get rid of the ropes that hold me. The desire to free me and to seize the knife begins to form in my whole being. I want to cut the witchdoctor's and the Italian's throat. I want to tear Jérôme's eyes out of their sockets. We're both struggling to get hold of the knife with our teeth like two wild dogs. It hurts! It hurts! It hurts!

–Guelele lele lele lele lele lele lele leeeeeeeeeeee!

Death. Pain. I want to kill. I see everything red. I thirst for blood, for the blood of Jéjé, who won't stop screaming. He looks at me with infinite hatred behind his war paintings. He wants to kill me too. Our mouths are full of foam, and we do not stop screaming. I can't catch the knife. The sorcerer kicks us apart. We crawl back to the knife.

–Guelele lele lele lele lele lele lele leeeeeeeeeeee!

The pain is unbearable. It makes me forget the knife. I keep screaming. My screams and Jérôme's ones only increase the pain. I am in a fetal position. I close my eyes. Scenes of death flash before my mind like in a black and white movie. I am tired of screaming. I shut up, and the pain subsides. We both fall silent. We hear each other breathing heavily. I don't know where I am. Everything is dark. I'm alone in a dark room. I look at my hands. They are children's hands. They are not tied. I am in a dark room. My parents have punished me. It is unfair. I hate them. I'm going to kill myself, and they'll see. I'll set the house on fire. I've never felt like this before. So full of hate. It's not me. So full of hate. It's not me. So full of hate. It's not me.

–Guelele lele lele lele lele lele lele leeeeeeeeeee!

I open my eyes and find Jérôme's almost out of their sockets. We sweat heavily. Jérôme utters in a voice that is not his own:

-JE* *SUIS* *LE* *DIABLE*!*

Without thinking and almost in unison, I exclaim before collapsing:

-I AM* *SATAN*!*

...

17 New Moon

–Guelele lele lele lele lele lele lele leeeeeeeeeee!

I am the cursed one. I am the lonely one. My punishment is the present. I am master and lord of the instant, and the instant does not exist. It disappears at birth. I have no memory. I only hate. Time only exists to be my prison. Yesterday and tomorrow are concepts I no longer understand. Men do not stop thinking about them.

They don't stop talking about God either, but they believe more in me than in Him. My tool is fear. God is not in the present. It must be the only place that exists devoid of His presence. God is. I remain to be, and I know, but I am not. I do not understand either what are the feelings that move men so much.

What senseless animals! To not be bored, they enthrone futility; when one wears out, they choose another to enthrone. They cling to life without realizing that it is also their prison. They do not know that, when they are alive, they are my only company. They do not understand that the only way they can get rid of my hatred is to stop living. They are my lost memory replacement, and the more they suffer or enjoy, the richer the memory, the fuller the instant. They don't know what escapes me when one of them dies, especially if he is old.

I would also like to die and finally escape from the instant, this eternal prison, this invisible chain. If I were to do away with them all, only the animals would be left. I am alone. The legends of my fall say that I had brothers in heaven before I fell. They also say that I rebelled against God. I remember nothing. I am innocent, by absolute amnesia. I must give credence to the stories of men. If the stories have changed throughout men's lives, I don't remember either, but I keep searching. I search because I don't have much else to do either.

To know without having a memory is something that the vast majority of men do not achieve. There are some alive. Some also see me, but they never reach me, even though I live in all of them. I am Legion, and I am the same. They all pass by my house. I am pure potential.

A few I do not have access to, their peers remember what it has cost them to get to that state. Others have arrived more quickly. They call them crazy or enlightened, but the crazy ones I manage to influence when they temporarily let go of their madness.

I have many names. I am the dark king. I hate. I am alone. The memory of men is short. I force them to leave traces, and they forget their meaning. I own the present, and being everything is almost nothing. They all come to me in the same way. Their peers build them the cage to make them fit for my influence. The day I invented morality must have been a great day. I wonder how I would preserve that concept if I had to invent it again.

One of them said, "I think. Therefore I am". I only think, I do not exist, only through creatures. I must try to invent morality in other animals. Man is very unstable. He is the best I have, but I find it hard to make him evolve much further than he has come. I am the dark king. I hate. I am alone.

I see one of those I can't touch. He is in a room full of candles. He is dressed in white. Old bearded man, I've seen you before. I don't remember you, but others know who you are and remember you. Don't come close to me! Don't disturb me in my bitter loneliness; I am the dark king!

–Guelele lele lele lele lele lele lele leeeeeeeeeee!

I am thirsty. I am very thirsty. I am afraid. I am cold. My life hurts. I have seen the dark king. I have been the dark king. I see the knife. I see Jerome. I see the sorcerer and the Italian. I love them. I pity them. I must kill them. Jérôme goes for the knife. I will take it first. We are both exhausted. It hurts to move. I am afraid. I'm cold.

–Guelele lele lele lele lele lele lele leeeeeeeeeee!

I can't stop crying. Neither can Jérôme. Chinamano takes the knife and frees us from our bonds. The two of us melt in a long embrace, and our fear is gone.

–You have been in a trance for exactly seven minutes, - says Tavola, - and of course, you have seen the dark king. Don't tell anything today. Let your memory settle down.

–It was terrible, Jéjé. I really would have killed you.

–Me too, *mon petit père*. Fortunately, Giorgio has tied firm knots.

–I had never seen, let alone suffered such powerful hypnosis, not even with drugs. I am stupefied, Mr. Tavola - I comment. I have already regained control of my person, and my breathing is normal. I am even strangely relaxed.

–You are not finished yet. Take the sheets of paper and write down your memories.

We reach for the sheets and pens to hold our story. I clutch my pen as if it were a tree branch. Jéjé does the same.

–I don't know... I can't...

–Neither do I!

–What's going on, guys?

–I forgot how to write! I can't write!

–Me neither! What's going on, Giorgio? What's going on!

We break out in cold sweats at the enormity of the event. We are both with the pens with far less skill than babies. I can't visualize the shape of the letters in my head. I can't grip the pen with my fingers. It falls out of my hands at every attempt. Stupefied, we both look at the sorcerer who is holding a mug of beer.

–Spit inside the beer. - says Tavola, and we listen to him, totally disoriented. - Stare daddy China in the eyes.

Chinamano, smiling, pours the entire contents of the jar over his head.

–Guelele lele lele lele lele lele lele leeeeeeeeeee!

–The pen thing is a final test. Hahaha! You should see each other's faces! Come on, you can write now. Write your names, and Chinamano will give you a blessing of long life.

–You may think it's very funny, Giorgio. But I'm a journalist. You almost scared me more than the dark king!

We are both a mess and white as a whitewash. My heart is racing again like a train of sheer terror. I am relieved to see that I know how to write again. While I am writing my name, Chinamano addresses me, and I look at Tavola asking for a translation.

–He says don't waste your time trying to put order into what can't be ordered. He says that he knows you, that he knows that you err in logic. If you want to move forward, you must feel the irrational, losing the desire to understand it. Like with the law of desire, you only get what you want when you stop wanting it. He also says that he likes you, that he has seen you both living together in a foreign land, and that you are sincere friends.

–Please tell him that I thank him for the lesson and that it will be hard for me to forget the dark king.

–He says he does not give lessons. No one gives them. These are only learned or not learned. He wishes you long life and tells you both that you will not remember the dark king until the next moon as soon as you leave the room. You will never forget him again. You will know that death stalks you when you forget to write again. It will be his way of saying goodbye to you forever.

We get ready in the suite's bathroom, and we go to meet our muses, who get a good scare when they see our looks. We only remember the knife scene and losing consciousness. The relief we both feel is such that we take it as a joke, and we are ready to go back to the party. When we arrive at the gallery, Silvia and Jéjé get sweet, and I propose to Lucia that we go back to our box at La Scala to charge me for all the ear pulling.

We are going towards La Scala, and almost all the dancers are masked. Some couples of actors and actresses in lycra are circulating, wearing a sign on their backs with an arrow pointing to their butts and a brief statement: "you can play, fast and with love". There is a discreet atmosphere of light orgy. Carlo gets the crowd up, forcing the back and forth of the surround sound to the maximum and calling the musicians walking through the crowd dressed in white. It's already dawn outside, and the session won't last much longer.

Lucia and I spent about an hour rubbing in our corner. Caresses, kisses, secrets, and still no promises. The awkwardness of the first moments always has a childhood flavor. Carlo starts to clearly announce the end with the usual cut and the usual encore. After the final bombshell, he is left in charge of the light music to set the mood at a very soft volume throughout the room until the last one comes out.

We are told that breakfast will be served in the gallery. We both stop by the bathroom to freshen up a bit and return to our table, where we find Chloé reading the newspaper. The table is full of pastries, and waiters come and go with jugs of coffee, tea, and juice.

–Welcome back, lovebirds. I have everything ready for you. If lady and gentleman want anything else, just call Tele-Chastity.

–You nasty girl. Where did the Yankee go?

–He turned green with the joint and went off to find his destiny. He was somewhat feeble for an elite athlete. - She says, putting down the newspaper and sipping his juice.

We settled in for breakfast. It's all very tasty. Chloé tells us about her conversation with Ronald and her impressions. She also emphasizes how surprised she was by his questions about what he was interested in learning about France. Nothing that a priori could call our attention in a first visit, such as the *Stade de France* or the artificial harbor of Normandy D-Day, specifically the artificial harbor, skipping everything else. He also wanted to know if we eat French fries with mayonnaise, as Travolta says.

–When I go back to France I'm going to visit my parents and convince them to spend a weekend in their little cottage in Libourne. They bought it when I was a child and all these years they insisted on keeping it without electricity or running water. For them, it was a way of getting back to mother earth. It was always a nuisance because the fireplaces and oil lamps are not enough to spend the nights in winter. I remember the old wool mattresses, the horrible chamber pot under the bed so I wouldn't have to go out to the latrine in the garden—the smell of oil from the lamps… The only thing I loved was that we ate everything cooked on firewood.

–I suppose you have a good supply of cheeses, - I ask. I've learned in your country that the only thing better than good cheese is a lot more cheese!

–There are good cheesemakers in the area and the best wines in the world. There you can still get them at a reasonable price by buying directly from the wineries. If you let me know in advance, you are invited. Now I regret not having enjoyed the potty and the oil lamps in time. My parents have given up the mother earth thing because of their ailments and have put the complete installation. It is a shame to see the plasma TV covering the old chimney!

–We can always make a bonfire in the garden. How is the garden?

–It is neither small nor big, but my mother has it very well kept. It has its vegetable garden, and there's room to play crocket or bocce. There's also a shed with an old Mini Austin from the sixties. Dad swears and swears decades ago that one day he's going to restore it.

–I think, Jeanne, that what we are going to organize for you is a blind date. Do you have any single friends, you little shrink? Look, the coif thing gives a lot of play.

–We can find a candidate, yes. Do you always carry your cap with you?

–Hahaha! No, you fools! You don't know what a problem it was to find a solution. The bonnet was still manageable with a white cloth and safety pins, but the tunic almost forced us to delay everything.

It is already full daylight. There are still quite a few people left for the time it is, and a cleaning crew is taking care of letting us know that things are not going to stretch any longer. We pick up our stuff in the closet, and I assume that I will not sleep with Lucia today. Anyway, we are exhausted, and we have made an appointment to have dinner together in the evening by candlelight.

Some friendly hostesses are handing out pins with the newspaper's logo and the year as we leave.

–They are made of silver. No one who did not stay for breakfast will have the pin. Take care of it, that's how you wear it on the 25th anniversary.

–Thank you very much, Miss. If we survive five more years, we'll bring it back. It was a bombastic party.

The three of us did not stay much longer in front of the square. I usually try to get back from parties before sunrise. It wasn't my rule before I was thirty, but I'm a very light sleeper, and if I go to bed in daylight, my circadian cycle goes off, and it takes me a whole week to get it back. I have a friend in America who randomly sends me some melatonin pills that help me a lot on these occasions. In exchange, I send him Jabugo ham in vacuum packs when I can. On more than one occasion, it has delighted customs agents instead of my friend. They are becoming increasingly savvy there at the airport.

18 Κάθαρσις

Five years have passed, but I remember those moments of deep despair as if it were happening all over again. Some early mornings, I have woken up with cold sweats and shortness of breath, thinking that the panic scenes were being replayed again in my room. Whenever it happens, Lucia reassures me with a hug and a kiss on my forehead.

–The same dream again, you crazy shrink? It's over, Spaniard, it's over. Go back to sleep and dream about us.

We were leaving the Vittorio Emanuele Gallery after the best anniversary party I have ever heard of. At least, that's how it has remained engraved in my memory. That day I met Lucia. Chloé, Lucia, and I were saying good night to each other at the entrance door, and the Duomo square was already full of life at 8:12 AM that Saturday in May. My head was spinning. We had all been drinking like crazy.

The day was clear and windless. A dog began to howl, then another. All the pigeons in the square took flight in a black swirl right under our noses. If the sun hadn't been in the sky, you might have thought they were bats. The ground began to shake. First, slightly, as if the Scala had resumed activity or a subway car passing under our feet. Then a little stronger. I looked at Lucia and Chloé, and it seemed as if the lines of their faces were blurring in electrostatic interference. I lost track of time until we heard a shriek coming out from the gallery.

–It's like in L'Aquila! It's happening again! Earthquake! Everybody to the square! To the square! To the square! Earthquake!

People began to run in panic towards the Duomo square, shouting and pushing and shoving. I took Silvia and Chloé's hand and followed the human tide. I was not the one running. I remember very well the sensation of turning my head a couple of times to see pieces of the crumbling dome raining down on the mob like a deadly snowfall of glass shards. My feet were moving forward on their own, and I was straining to squeeze hard on the hands of the girls struggling to free themselves.

Once we reached the square center where everyone was converging, anguish's feeling did not fade. We all looked up to the sky wishing with all our strength that we could grow wings to follow the pigeons that were watching us from the air. Groups of three or four began to form, kneeling and holding each other by the shoulders. Silvia kept shouting. Chloé began to pray the Lord's Prayer in French, and my fear had silenced me. We were joined by an elderly couple who must have been out for a morning walk, and the woman accompanied Chloé's prayer in Italian. The man couldn't make a sound out of his throat either and was blinking very rapidly.

The five of us were hugging each other and paralyzed by terror. In the circle we formed, it was impossible to distinguish whether the tremor was coming from the earth, from our neighbors' bodies, or from within ourselves. All around us, the same expression of disbelief on people's faces. Some few were running without direction and stumbling. Others were directly lying on the ground. Many were crying.

At 8:27 AM, the earthquake tore the Duomo square floor and opened a crack of several tens of meters along Corso Vittorio Emanuele, up to the center of the square. Four people lost their lives falling through it. Fortunately, no residential buildings were affected.

The opening of the sinkhole marked the end of the tremors abruptly. Only people could be heard sobbing. I could see those lying, collapsed on the ground, and rescued by their immediate neighbors. Our circle then turned into a tight embrace, completely crowded together. We breathed in unison. Lucia and I looked at each other as I wiped away her tears, and she strangled my abdomen. She had lost her shoes, and the makeup smeared around her beautiful eyes reddened from crying made the scene even more tragic.

Another tremor was heard, this time of a different nature, like a dull, distant echo. Lucia and Chloé curled up on my lap as we watched the cathedral's stained glass windows explode, and a cloud of fine white dust flew out of the openings. The cathedral's roof was collapsing on the inside. The old couple was holding each other, and all the while, Chloé had not stopped praying.

The rain of debris inside the cathedral stopped. The structure of the Duomo held firm. Only a few blocks of stone had broken off from the vaults. The replacement of the marble surface is still in progress. The stress had evaporated all alcohol from our bodies. Many were vomiting. There was a silence interrupted by the first sirens of the few ambulances and police cars that were beginning to approach the area.

–Are you okay? Are you both okay? - I asked.

–I think so, - replied Chloé, inspecting her whole body with both hands.

–My ankle hurts, - said Lucia, sniffling, - Is it over? Tell me it's over!

–It seems to be over, yes. Your ankle is not broken. Stay seated, Lucia. Don't move from here for a moment. I'm going to see if I can help that child with a hissy fit. Are you all right, gentlemen? - I asked the couple. She answered.

–Thank heaven, son. Thank heaven. My husband suffers from heart disease, you know? Francesco, take a deep breath. Thank heaven you just took the pill. Take a deep breath, and don't get upset, Francesco. Count to a hundred. Are you all right?

–It seems so. Do not leave the square until the security services come. It is the safest place in case of an aftershock.

My only clue was to reassure the couple and the girls. The only earthquakes I had ever seen in my life had been from the comfort of the sofa or the cinema seat. Since that day, I get a lump in my throat when I see a scene on the screen. I have done a lot of research on the subject. It is not the same to study fear to work with those who suffer from it than to feel how it invades every pore of your skin and every cell of your body. I have developed a deep empathy for victims of natural disasters that I never had before.

Thomas J. Scheff is an eminent scholar in the study of social psychology. He argues that emotions are not a cultural product but a human body tool to deal with painful situations. Thus, crying, for example, would be a biological necessity. Babies are born crying, and what culture teaches is to repress crying, sometimes through punishment. This accumulation of cultural impositions to close natural escape valves would be the origin of chronic stacks of stress with deplorable results for people's ability to relate to each other.

The fact is that, in a moment like the one we experienced that morning, there was no room for any cultural barriers. Everybody was united under the same emotion and showed themselves with their true selves. It has often been said that human beings have a natural tendency to do good, and it certainly seemed that way. The little boy was shrieking and breathing unconnectedly. I grabbed him in a firm embrace and began to whisper a tango in his ear, rocking him like a mother rocks her child. Gradually, the boy regained a regular breathing rhythm, and, holding him in arms, I brought him close to Lucia. He must have been about seven years old, but he instinctively put his thumb to his mouth. I remembered my son Luis.

–Look, girls, I've met a beautiful boy. Look, little boy, I'm going to introduce you to two great friends. They're both extraordinary.

–Hello, little boy, I'm Chloé. He is a very handsome boy, isn't he?. This one here is called Lucia. What's your name?

–My name is Jacopo. Why are you talking with your mouth full? - He said, wiping away his tears.

–Hahaha! My mouth is not full, Jacopo. I'm French, and French girls talk like this. Lucia is Italian. Say hello to Jacopo Lucia.

–Hi Jacopo, don't be afraid, it's over. Do you want me to hold you in my arms? Where are your parents? - Jacopo leaves with Lucia.

–I don't know, they were buying things, and I was playing with the pigeons, and then everything started shaking.

–Do you know your mother's phone number, Jacopo? What is your mother's name? - I asked

–I have it here on the medal. Her name is Norma. - I look at it and quickly dial the number, a woman answers.

–Hello, who is it? – I could feel her speeding up.

–Hello Norma. You can calm down. Your son is safe. We are in the square a short distance from the cathedral. Are you all right?

–Bless you! Lucca, they've found the child! Don't hang up. We're on our way.

Soon, Jacopo's parents show up, and the mother inspects him as if checking that everything is in place. They all stay with us while I decide to call Sandra. It takes her a while to pick up, but finally, I hear her voice over the loudspeaker.

–Sandra. Are you all right? Where are you?

–Of course, I'm fine. We're at Pietro's house. Is something wrong?

–Something wrong? Switch on a television. We are in the square in front of a crack the size of a train. There has been an earthquake.

–So that's what the shaking was. We thought it was the construction site across the street. It didn't look like an earthquake here. Are you all right? Are you with the girls?

–We are the three of us, yes. We're all right. Give the phone to Pietro. Lucia wants to talk to him. I'll be calmer. We'll talk later, you and I.

–Pietro, turn on the TV and pick up the phone! There's been an earthquake!

I give Lucia the phone and decide to move if she can walk on her bad ankle. A little later, I try to talk to Jérôme without success. The lines are down. The ankle thing is not severe, and we slowly make our way towards the Castello Sforzesco to try to get out of there.

What do you do after an event like this? Do you get as far out of town as quickly as possible and without suitcases? Do you give a speech? Do you find a hospital? Do you file a report? It's like being a first-time parent. There are no manuals that helpfully prepare you for it. In our case, after the scare and thanks to a providential cab driver, we decided to go home and try to get some sleep.

The aftermath was not as atrocious as it could have been had the earthquake been of greater magnitude or if the crack had collapsed a residential building. Each of the four deceased was mourned by the whole country. The proximity of the tragedy in L'Aquila only increased affection and solidarity with the families of those absent. Many more were injured. The medical services treated Forty-six amidst the cracking, the disbanding, and the glass of the dome. Nine people were seriously disabled.

That morning, newspapers had already hit the streets before the earthquake, and many mentioned the celebration with glee. A couple of them openly criticized the laxity of authorities for having allowed a national monument to be used to celebrate a private event, as significant as it was. These media took advantage of the tragedy to make more noise about it, and Jérôme was forced to defend his position in a televised debate.

–Do you realize that without your anniversary party, far fewer people would have been injured? - He was asked.

–I am perfectly aware of this. I pressed the button that shook the earth as the icing on the cake. Aren't you ashamed of yourselves for wanting to arrogate to us the misfortune of those affected?

–We simply wonder why anyone can afford to close the Vittorio Emanuele Gallery for partisan purposes.

–Listen well. I know that you earn a salary that requires you to utter aberrations all day long. You're not bad at it. I may even consider your resume if you trade your aberrations for real content. Our anniversary was agreed upon with authorities, and all relevant licenses were properly issued. Second point: at no time was political support expressed for any party of the parliamentary arc, except for a dramatization conceived for the occasion, about a non-existent party. Last point: it was in the city's interest to carry out the filming to promote tourism abroad. It turns out that, because of the earthquake, a documentary is being made with the material of that night. It will be of international reach, and its funds will be added to those already existing for L'Aquila. I will not answer any more insidious questions.

Until then, Jéjé was just another citizen. From then on, he became a public figure in Italy. The controversy was substantial, but it served to feed the feeling of solidarity in the country. When it comes to pain, one can forget about quarrels about boundaries, accents, or goats; even more so when it comes to our old continent, an expert in intrigues and disagreements.

The crack is still open today. Local authorities decided it should remain a memorial, and today it is one more emblem of the city. Graffiti artists are allowed to express themselves on it, and its message has changed over the years. It is reminiscent of the Berlin Wall before its demolition. The wall of discord today rests in millions of pieces in the shrines of so many homes, while the crack is still alive and leads anyone who sees it to meditate on the transience of life.

The Duomo's domes are being completed by the same team that recently finished the Sagrada Familia in Barcelona. We Spaniards had lost hope with Gaudi's monument, but finally, it was achieved, and today the magnificent cathedral is finished. We have not yet returned to Milan. Somehow, it is as if we were waiting for them to finish repairing the roof of their magnificent monument.

Today Lucia and I are married and live in Portugal. A perfect compromise for our two Latin languages. I found northern Italy too cold and Palermo too far away from the airport hubs, to which I am still a slave. She still works with her father and has set up a leather store here. I must confess that, despite loving Sicily almost as much as she does and being a fan of pasta with sea urchin and swordfish, as well as *cannoli*, I could never get used to *milza*. On the other hand, she didn't want to settle in Madrid because she said she wanted to be near the sea since leaving Milan. I had always told her that once you get used to the Atlantic, the Mediterranean turns into a salt lake.

Luis, my son, has reached the legal age to choose to come and live with me. Lucia did not mind the idea, and today the three of us are building our notion of happiness in a beautiful little house in Setubal. All four of us. Lucia has been growing Martina, our future daughter, in her belly for five months. I hope she inherits her mother's eyes.

19 Euro-trash

Sandra and Pietro had left the party at a moment when their sensual evolutions on the dance floor had reached the maximum temperature. Without saying goodbye, between laughter and furtive caresses, they took a cab that brought them to pick up Pietro's car at the door of Lucia's house and went to Pietro's house. Sandra did not want to risk the possibility of the four of us crossing paths in Fatebenefratelli and was also curious to know how a European duke, forty years old and single, lives.

They had their first kiss going up the elevator. When they reached the landing, it took Pietro a long time to find the door key groping in his pockets. He also tried to make as little noise as possible so that his mother would not spoil the moment, although he knew well that the lady was sleeping so soundly that not even a neutron bomb would wake her from her sleep, it was better not to risk it.

The apartment where Pietro lived had a rather stately, old-fashioned décor with light, well-chosen modernity touches. A few busts scattered around the hallways accompanied an eclectic mix that included, among others, Kandinski and Jack Roberts. The canopy of the bed was presided over by a curious selection of mythological beasts made by various Italian authors' pencils. A pot-bellied root-wood chest of drawers watched over them in front of the bed, dressed in several Egyptian cotton thread layers. They made devoted love until well into the morning.

Neither of them had given much importance to the earth tremor, busy as they were in getting to know every corner of their bodies. When Leonardo called Sandra on the phone, they were just getting ready for a nap. They watched the news for about ten minutes while Pietro sent some SMS to Sicily, Madrid, and Bordeaux, as Lucia had asked him to say that they were all well, and they went to rest.

They had not slept two hours when Pietro's mother opened the heavy curtains and turned on the bedroom light.

–Wake up, you slacker! I've been ringing the doorbell for half an hour and no response! The Prime Minister has been working for hours in his office, and you're sleeping like a pig! Shame on you! What a shitty race! I want you to come and watch the news with me!

–Mamma, I've seen them! How many times do I have to tell you that you can't come in like that without permission? I'm going to condemn that door!

The woman had not noticed Sandra's presence until she stuck her head out from under the sheet. As soon as she saw her, standing there in front of the bed, she threw off the blanket and, dressed in her cat-like nudity, got up to greet the visitor.

–Good morning! You must be Mrs. Carola. I am Sandra Gómes, *muito prazer*. Pietro and Lucia have told me a lot about you. How is your stomach this morning?

Sandra planted two resounding kisses on his cheeks, stroking his head with her right hand and holding one hand with her left. She fixed her gaze on her with a disarming smile. Donna Carola was slow to react.

–Oh, wow! Well, it's my pleasure. It's my pleasure. Put something on, miss. You'll catch a cold, - muttered the old lady, arching both eyebrows.

–Pietro, let's watch the news with your mother, don't be inconsiderate. I'm sure she has delicious coffee, doesn't she? I'm going to take a shower.

Without waiting for an answer, she headed for the bathroom, wiggling softly and singing Roberto Carlos. Pietro was like his first name: petrified. It was the first time he had seen his mother not explode like a volcano.

–It's all right, sonny. I'm going to tell Antonietta that we have a guest... Don't be long.

–Of course, *mamma*, of course - Dona Carola disappeared in the dark down the corridor without saying "this mouth is mine".

He went into the bathroom. Sandra was still singing. They were both enchanted by each other. He trimmed his beard and took out the dresser drawer a pair of silk pajamas and a matching bathrobe. Sandra put on a bathrobe and high heels. In this guise, they went to the apartment across the lobby.

The living room table was set with a hearty breakfast. Sandra pounced on the pancakes with fig jam. The two of them commented on the party and the earthquake while Pietro's mother watched them in silence.

–How lucky we were, Pietro! Can you imagine if something happens to us? How awful! All those poor people. Sometimes we suffer things like that with the rains. Some landslides have killed many people. I escaped one by pure chance.

–Yes, here we are very affected by L'Aquila, it was terrible. You have already seen the images on television. They are broadcasting it live all over the planet. I don't know what's going on lately that everything is a misfortune. I even wonder if it wouldn't be wise to consider moving. It was a tiny breach. It could have been a full-blown earthquake, and that, in the heart of Milan, can be catastrophic.

–Look, don't be defeatist. You never know where the next disaster will strike. Maybe you'll lock yourself up in Sardinia, a tsunami will come, and the ground in Milan will never tremble again. You have to live with what you have.

–Well, I'll give it to you if it doesn't shake all day again. You look like you liked the pancakes.

–Mmmm. I love them. It's the jam. It's so natural. Where do you buy it?

–They make it in Antonietta's village and send it to us. This one must be more than six months old, but they have a little secret to make them last a whole year.

–Congratulations, Antonietta. It's delicious! I had a great time at the party. I liked Jérôme and his girlfriend. How crazy cute! Leo lived with him in Germany for a while. It looks like they had a good time together.

–Yes, very original. His idea of a Nomad Party is still going around in my head. Look, mom. Those from the red newspaper, as you call it, propose to make a party of expatriates. If you have lived or live outside your homeland, you are automatically entitled to a membership card, and it is the same party for all countries. You are very quiet. Are you all right?

Donna Carola came out of her silence. She had not stopped watching Sandra closely during the entire breakfast. Sandra did not seem the least bit bothered.

–Do you see how red they are? That's the Communist International in cybernetic version. I forbid you to buy that newspaper!

–But, *mamma*. They do not propose collectivization, the growth of the State's role, or the takeover of buildings. From my point of view, it is very international and very little communist. I see it more as a catalyst to integrate countries and get out of bipartisanship. The *Cirque du Soleil* of politics. I like it better than the parties that call themselves green and pick up the red remains you mention.

–Look, kiddo. I'm not going to argue with you out of respect for your guest. Did she like the jam? I'll give her two jars, so she remembers us. Are you passing through Spain? If you want to get to know Italy, I have no objection to lending you an apartment here in Milan or our house on the lake. It's up to you.

–Thank you very much, Mrs. Carola, how thoughtful of your mother, Pietro! I had never really thought of anything like that, but I thank you for your hospitality - she got up and gave her another kiss on the cheek -. Now, if you'll excuse me, I'm going to get dressed, I'm looking awful, and I'd like to go home to change my clothes and see if Leo is still in one piece.

Pietro couldn't get over his astonishment, although he didn't blink. As Sandra walked out the door, his mother put on another coffee. He did the same.

–Hey, *mamma,* are you going to tell me what the hell is wrong with you? It's not normal for you to be like this. Are you not going to criticize me for anything? I'm over forty years old, and you have no right to come into my room like that.

–There's nothing wrong with me, son. I'm very happy, that's all.

Donna Carola drank her coffee and got up from the table. Pietro had a feeling that his mother was up to something. It was not possible that knowing her as he did, she had not summoned all the monsters of the underworld when she saw Sandra. She had always been very racist, as well as classist.

After a short while, the old woman appeared with a bulky leather briefcase in her arms. It had to be quite ancient because the leather was dehydrated and cracked, and the cloth bands were entirely worn by the passing of the years. She left it on the table and sat down in her chair to put on another cup of coffee.

–What is this, Mom?

–That is something that was meant for your sister, but I have decided today to pass it on to you. Open it, open it.

Pietro carefully opened the bundle to try not to spoil it any more than it already was. Inside were some sorters, and in each sorter were grouped title deeds in Portuguese and Spanish.

–I don't understand, Mom. But you're going to explain it to me right now, am I wrong?

–You are not wrong. I am going to explain it to you, and you are going to pay close attention. These are land titles in Brazil, Argentina, Paraguay, and Bolivia. Some of them, as you can see, have been renewed for more than three hundred years. All of them, as of today, are in my name.

–Was Dad aware of this? He never said anything about us having investments from across the pond.

–Your father was like all the men in the family, a fool. He was always engrossed in the nobility of the shoe, like you. Poverty of spirit is what you all have - she looked him straight in the eye and spoke with a tone of authority -. The women of the family have bought these properties in favorable times in exchange for their best jewels. It is a tradition that has been passed from woman to woman ever since. No man that I know of has ever known about this. Has it ever surprised you that we don't have a collection of family jewels? Do you think I don't like diamonds?

Pietro was now losing his temper. He began to look more closely at the documents on the table. They were very old. He took pleasure in comparing the stamps, the signatures, the ink strokes written in pen, the seals.

–This is worth a lot today, Mom. Do you have a rough estimate of what's here in today's currency?

–I'm sure there's more than you can make in five lifetimes selling little shoes, you little punk! It's not about that. It's about why I'm giving this to you today. You're going to make some trips. You're going to put everything in your name with a power of attorney of mine.

–And why me, here and now?

–Because the circle has simply been closed. The message that has crossed the centuries in the mouths of your great-great-grandmothers refers to blood strength. Blood is the essential thing, Pietro, and it is already much diminished in our

European families. Titles were won on the battlefields and by conquering barren lands on the other side of the globe. You would not be able to spend three nights alone in the wilderness without melting in tears. Every once in a while, you have to reinforce the blood, and that girl is the sign that I would never have believed I would see with my own eyes.

–But Mom. I certainly like Sandra, but we hardly know each other. I don't know how much she likes me either.

–It will be her or someone else! But something tells me it will be her. It doesn't matter. The message says it in no uncertain terms: "*Blood, sister, when the first male of the family crosses the threshold of your door on the arm of an unknown sister from across the sea, you must reveal the secret. Only then, for that will be the unmistakable sign that, by its force, blood has crossed the ocean again to take our name with it. Then the fruit of your loins must take possession of those lands and build a new branch of the old tree on that continent of promise.*"

–Mamma...

–You don't need to say anything to that girl. I will do my duty, and you will do yours. I won't say anything to your brothers either. They will only know about this operation when they read the will, and I am gone. I hope you leave the blessed little shoes to your brother and leave all those fierce great-great-grandmothers who have been preparing your destiny in a good place. I'm very proud of you, son. And don't forget: she has all the cards to be the good one. Listen to this old woman who knows very well what she's talking about. It's very serious nonsense.

Pietro stood up and tucked the documents under his arm. He kissed his mother on the forehead and staggered back to his apartment. He left the legacy he had just received in his office and sat down on a sofa to reflect. He was not so impressed that his mother had seen in Sandra the sign women in the family had been waiting for so long. He was much more amazed that they had managed to keep it hidden throughout history with the tribulations his people had gone through, especially in the two world wars. The secondary role he attributed to women was crumbling by the minute. I also had no idea that any adventurous ancestors had ever made the Americas. Sandra appeared through the office door.

–Can you call me a cab, *duquezinho*? I hate repeating clothes. Hey, your mother doesn't look like the ogre Lucia was painting. She invited me to Milan and everything. Do you think she was serious?

–There's no way you're going by cab. Wait for me, and I'll take you. It sounds like she was serious, yes. I don't know what happened to you. It's like you put a spell on her.

–No way, pretty boy. You stay here quietly and rest. If you want to be gallant, I can consider dinner with you tonight - he bit Pietro's neck and spoke in his ear -. Dinner and everything else, cat. I liked it very much.

–I liked it a lot too. You're a tropical storm. I'm not going to let you turn down my car ride.

–Don't insist. I feel like seeing Milan by myself, even if it's just for a little while.

–All right. I'll call you in the afternoon, *bellissima*. I promise you surprises.

He hailed a cab and escorted her to the street. He was still in an uproar about his mother. He spied Sandra out of the corner of his eye and imagined himself emulating Robinson Crusoe with the tremendous brunette and no hope of rescue as he rubbed his chin. When the car got lost at the end of the street, he bit his ring and went upstairs to lie down.

20 Aftermath

Luisito is at school, and we decided to spend the day in Tomar, near Santarém, to visit the convent of Christ. The monument is a Templar fortress to which modules were added until it became a religious residence. Lucia is sleeping in the back seat, and I am listening to a Fito & Fitipaldis record. Good rock and roll always puts me in a good mood. I guess Martina is backing me up from Lucia's belly, and I'm enjoying the scenery. It's a perfect day, a little wind rocking the car in certain viaducts, and sunny as hell.

The Iberian Peninsula is a history book especially marked by the reconquest. The inhabitants of Porto, still today, call *mouros* those of Lisbon and further south. Portugal is very green and diverse, despite the infection of eucalyptus that invades its mountains. The eucalyptus is an exceptionally demanding tree in its demand for water. This voracity means that its forest companions end up dying of thirst if the climate is not humid. Some areas of the landscape would be a perfect habitat for koalas if one day the species had to be protected and, as there are no apes in Europe - at least not arboreal ones - we could see something more than squirrels or birds in the branches.

I have always thought Castile suffers a millenary curse. You don't need a border marker or any sign to know if you are in one country or the other. If you go east and there is no more green, you are in Spain. "Wide is Castile", says the popular expression of old, which somehow expresses "anything goes". Wide, brave, and full of nooks and crannies and character. Epics are not written from the comfort of Eden. The fact is that, for the Portuguese, Castile has historically been a bit like the eucalyptus: it is possible to collaborate, but without stepping on each other's toes.

This forced coexistence between Portugal and Spain has given the Portuguese a very particular pragmatism. Undoubtedly, a great part of the Portuguese cultural richness lies in the fact that they have wisely integrated many of the good things proscribed in Spain throughout the centuries, purifying some bad ones. The best proof of this was demonstrated the day Napoleon planted his army on the border and sent a message to Portugal's king: "Are you our friends?" The short man from Ajaccio was always very captious. If they declared themselves friends, they kept the country, but the English, military masters of the sea, would make them lose the same sea's commercial supremacy. If they declared themselves hostile, war math would make them lose Portugal.

Faced with such an existential and material dilemma, King João did not hesitate for a second. "Wait a little while, Mr. Bonaparte. I'm thinking about it." And, neither short nor lazy, he moved the Portuguese empire's capital and his entire court to Rio de Janeiro, thus maintaining the economic cohesion of the empire and sitting comfortably to watch the corpse of his enemy pass by. Today's Brazil owes much to the Braganza family since then. Compared to that of the rest of the Latin American countries, its emancipation was exemplary. The immense territory that Portugal won by chance from Spain in Tordesillas remains to this day.

The convent of Christ is magnificent. Before walking up the steep path that leads to the top, we take a walk through the village, which abounds everywhere the crosses of the Order of the Temple. Everything is Templar here: the pharmacy, the bar in the square, the greengrocer on the corner. If there are any warrior monks of the Holy Sepulchre left, they can certainly be dispatched here. Lucia insists on walking up for the sake of her pregnancy. I am a little apprehensive, and we stop several times along the way with the excuse of taking pictures of the wonderful scenery.

Arriving at the main gate in the fortress wall, we see a sign with the building's plan. The most curious thing is the pentagonal tower, which unfortunately is not open to the public. There is a lot of mystique in numbers. In the case of number five, the most apparent analogy when talking about Templars is the five letters that form Jerusalem. We must not forget that Hebrew is a language of consonants. We head to the entrance and begin our visit through the cloisters. The cloister I admire most is the one at Mont Saint-Michel. These are also thought-provoking.

Four elements attract our attention during the visit, in this order: The original tower, the Manueline façade, the kitchens, and the monks' rooms. We stop for a long time at the tower, trying to breathe the mystery of the place and its history. The tower is an immense polygonal tube presided in its center by eight stone arches forming an inner turret. It has, attached to one wall, a single wooden rod with the same shape as the traditional organs' metal ones.

–This whistle in here must reverberate throughout the valley - I tell my wife - I'd love to hear it in action.

It reminds me of the Teatro Massimo shape in Palermo, which is also a tube. This must have phenomenal acoustics. There, music gets to your ears without any kind of amplification. I shall show you someday.

–It's true, I've never been there. I've only gotten to see its facade, which is where the ending of the third part of "The Godfather" was filmed.

The Manueline façade looks like something straight out of a Moebius drawing. The column on the right is particularly amusing because a belt girds it with a perfectly carved buckle. It gives the impression that this buckle is the support for the rest of the structure and that, if it were to come loose, the whole structure would collapse.

When we get to the kitchens, I think of Silvia, Jéjé's wife. Silvia is always looking for atypical places to organize her conventions, and she was going to love this one. Her husband would have to pull chestnuts out of the fire to get the permits. They now live in Geneva and have had two beautiful twin girls. In the end, Silvia didn't have to go through fertility treatment like her sister. The twins were totally by chance.

Jéjé decided to move to Switzerland as soon as he got support to form the Nomad Party. He was determined to found it because he took the Milan earthquake to heart. He was very annoyed by the way the newspaper had been attacked at the time. The *Giornale del Mondo* is now run by Niccolo, its former editor, and maintains the polemicist line initiated by his predecessor. The Nomad Party today governs in two Eastern European countries and has parliamentary representation in six others. Jérôme is still a working machine and has lost the poor lock of hair used to save his bald head. I am always careful not to remind him of this when we meet. The last time was in Paris, at *Le Trappiste*, as usual. He was going crazy with the preparations for the twins' birth and was still wearing the same black trench coat and cap. Now he was the one directly involved in the student protests. Every time we meet, we recall the dark king. When I returned to Madrid after the party, I had the handkerchief I had dried the mixture on my face analyzed. They only found cereal and natural pigments, not a trace of alkaloids or any element that could cause psychotropic effects. Today, I still wonder if the dark king's prison was not the shaman's head.

We leave the kitchen, to which I plan to bring Silvia to see if she is encouraged to ask for permission to roast some pork in that oven with the Belgian, in the Holy Inquisition fashion. Still today, I wonder how we can have the nerve to rebuke human sacrifices in the new world while lighting human pyres all over Europe. We pass through the refectory, where we find a pad of clues left there by some professor. On the printed paper, we see a portrait of Philip the second in which a brief description of his biography as king of Portugal is given, and the "treasure hunt" of the brave students is set in motion. Thus, because of Philip's marriage, the Portuguese also develop, in their childhood, a sense of ownership of the empire where the sun never set.

In the monastic rooms, better described as cells, we stop for a while to rest. The heating system they used is very particular. The cells are as austere as can be imagined in these cases. Three questions come to mind: What moves a human being to leave the secular life and lock himself up for the rest of his days in these cells? How did the one who, without any vocation, was forced to this lifelong confinement by simple order of birth? Would this be a resting point before facing the formidable journey to the new world? We both spent some time rambling on these subjects and remembered Chloé.

Chloé has not moved from Lyon during all this time. She has been living for a couple of years with Didier, a fellow countryman from

Aix-en-Provence. An actor with a very funny southern accent. They came to see us last year, and we had a lot of fun with them. After a few Port wine tastings at the bar in Chiado square, Didier confessed he owed his vocation to Asterix because of the scene in the Roman theater where the audience starts shouting, "*Assez, c'est une honte, on se moque du public!*" He said he had always wanted to be that actor.

We have a pending trip to Brazil to visit Sandra. She still lives in her hotel and has an intermittent relationship with Pietro, whom we only hear from when we talk to her. Pietro has passed the shoe factories to his brother and is moving closer to Mercosur. Lucia suspects he will end up living there and hopes so, for the sake of her ex's mental health, whose mother seems to have left him with an unforgettable memory.

As we stroll through the grapefruit trees in the convent's orchard, I can't help but email a photo of the tower to Michael, who is the one who introduced me to the Temple Church in London. After the visit, we set off back to Setubal. In all this time, we have learned that Portugal is a very special place to look for hidden restaurants, and in this case, I am not going to make an exception.

Following the signs indicating *Castelo do Bode*, we stopped at a camping area with a restaurant that offers a very nice view of the natural reserve and ordered some octopus and some lamb. We wash it down with local wine, Templar, and very appropriate to accompany the animal's compact meat. The maître tells us the tornado's story that devastated the region around the same time that the Duomo's crack opened. At the end of the meal, I receive Michael's answer on my phone.

"Hello Leonard, I see you're digging into the history of the Knights Templar, so our encounter wasn't entirely useless. Keep studying. It never ends, as I always tell you. I am enclosing an extract from a hypnosis session with a patient who has been claiming for years to be Jacques de Molay. I have always liked the classics like Napoleon or Julius Caesar, but this one is very original. A big hug and congratulations on the little girl that is coming to you. Come and see me any day now.
A big hug,
M."

I open the attachment and start reading it aloud to Lucia:
–Stare at the pendulum. Do not lose sight of the pendulum. When I say three, you will fall into a pleasant sleep. One, two, three! You are sleeping soundly. What do you hear around you?

–Wailing can be heard. Metallic knocks. More wailing.

–How does your body feel?

–I can hardly feel it. Pain. I'm hanging on a wall. I only feel pain in my wrists. They hurt so much it feels like I have no hands. More pain. Every heartbeat bounces off my ribs and my feet. It hurts so much!

–What's around you?

–I see straw on the floor. I see a prisoner hanging on the opposite wall. Moans come from his mouth. It's Hugues! It's Hugues!

–Who are you?

–Hugues! It's Jacques de Molay! We are in a cell of the Holy Inquisition! Now I remember. They've been torturing us for days! May they break all my bones, but not the water again! Hugues, hold on! Remember that we come here to die! Tell them what they want to hear about the cult, and let's leave this world at once! Tell them that the treasure is in the land of the crescent!

–What does Hugues answer?

–He asks me where the treasure really is. I don't know, Hugues. The last ship sailed from Lisbon last month towards the new land. It's a lot of gold. It's all gold! When the time and the hour come,s it will serve to build a happy country far from the demons of Avignon. Damn their souls, traitors!

–What new land?

–Hughes, your judgment is clouded. I'm talking about Nova Atlantis! You know that there is a plan, you know that we will take revenge on this pope! You know very well that, in our Promised Land, there will be no place for those who dirty St Peter's sandals! And they won't have to dig up the land to master the oceans! All the gold, Hugues! Do you realize that?

–What about King Philip?

–The damned Capets will be taken care of by their people. Remember the scroll of the Holy City, Hugues. The force of blood! Those peasants are a mixture of barbarians and Latins. They are still like beasts, but they learn to read before the others. You administer all the schools on the continent. You know the weaknesses and virtues of each people. They will take care of the Capettos! I dreamt it tonight, Hugues!

–Who knows where the treasure is?

–Hughes! Geoffroy! My whole body hurts! I can't take it anymore! Not the water again! I spit out the cross! I'll confess! I'll confess! I'll confess!

–Calm down. You're sound asleep again. Take a deep breath. You feel profound relief. Count to one hundred. When you reach fifty-five, you will open your eyes and remember nothing. You will be in a perfect state. Start counting. One, two, three...

I finish reading, and Lucia pours us the last glass of wine. Laughing, we promise to go to London on our next vacation so she can meet the pirate with the cat on his shoulder. I feel like strolling through its parks and getting fond of tea again. What I will never repeat is an opera at the National Theatre. I almost lost sense when I had to swallow La Traviata translated into English. "*Be happy and raise your glass*", they sang at the *Libiamo*. There are limits to everything, even to fusion.

We went for a walk along the edge of the forest. It is a magnificent landscape, and the walk is ideal for digesting the lamb. Lucia is carrying an old-fashioned umbrella. She loves them and has a hard time finding them because nowadays only umbrellas or beach umbrellas are sold in this format. She uses it as a support to walk along the rocks until we reach a landing. Before we sit down, we look at the landscape, and another memory strikes me.

–Do you remember the madman in the Duomo? He should have been hypnotized too. He had a thousand cosmogonies in his head.

–I remember from what Chloé told me, yes. He looked terrible. I think Martina kicks!

–I can't wait to see her out.

–Hey, you're a shrink. You love archetypes, don't you?

–I don't dislike them at all. Why?

Lucia points to the ground with her finger. When I look between my feet, she is finishing, with a clean stroke of the tip of her umbrella, the silhouette of a heart. I look into those eyes that hold the whole universe, and we both melt in an endless kiss.

THE END

EPILOGUE

–Wake up, Fritz! You can go now.

–Wolfram half-opened his eyes and saw the cell in which he had spent the night. He washed his face in the small yellowish sink in the corner and went out.

–What's the matter, officer? Can't even sleep comfortably in the barracks anymore?

–It happens that there has been an earthquake in the Duomo, and we have the worst day of the decade. It also happens that Giancarlo arrives in an hour and, if he sees you around here, he will probably want to do more than reprimand you. Your hit yesterday doesn't seem to have made him any fun. If he catches up with you, you won't get away with a good beating.

–Ach! An earthquake in the Duomo? Are you kidding me?

–Do I look like I'm joking? Get out now, and don't let me see you here again! We have methods for recalcitrants like you. You know that very well. Air!

He went out into the street. The morning was cool and sunny. He retraced his steps towards the center. It would take him at least an hour and a half to walk to the cathedral. At half past twelve, he could see the square from the barriers of the police cordon. It was deserted, but the sirens were coming and going aimlessly. Some passers-by were arguing with the *carabinieri* to try to get permission to see the wreckage.

Via Cappellari was unguarded, and he crept stealthily toward the cathedral. No one saw him reach the side. Through a shattered stained glass window, he slipped inside the temple. Most of the pews were completely splintered and covered with rubble. Huge blocks of stone had bombarded the floor and damaged the interior.

He looked up at the roof and saw the blue sky in a spectacle that only the builders of the last phase could have beheld before him. The image brought him to his knees. He crouched down in a beseeching attitude and stood there, completely motionless. Only the sirens could be heard passing from time to time.

A hinge on the front door creaked and clanked between the columns. He did not know how long he had been like that, but he said to himself that it was not good to be surprised by the forces of order again, and he went back through the same window through which he had entered. He was struck by the fact that no piece of stone had fallen on the pulpit through which he had fled from Giancarlo.

He started to walk without direction, and so, strolling through Milan with a blank mind, he watched the evening fall. He hadn't eaten anything all day, and his body didn't seem to complain about it either. He decided to stop by a gas station that had a shower for truckers and where he was known.

He asked for the shower keys and went in. He took off all his rags and washed his whole body with a bar of soap. He even chewed a piece of soap to clean his teeth. He trimmed his long hair and beard with a pair of scissors he carried in his jacket pocket after showering. He looked at himself for a long time in the mirror and stopped rolling his eyes forever. He rinsed the hair off his body, got dressed, and walked back towards the center.

It was getting dark when Wolfram took out of his pocket the ten Euros he had been given the day before at the cathedral. He looked for a phone booth of the kind used by immigrants and which now abounded in Milan. He asked for a booth and dialed a telephone number.

–Jawoll?

–Frida, is that you?

–Yes, this is Frida. Who is this?

–I am your brother. I need your help to get to Germany. I'm in Milan. Can you help me? I want to go back to university.

The phone remained silent on the other end of the line until a long sob was heard.

–I thought you were dead! Of course, I'm going to help you, asshole! Call back in half an hour, and I'll send you some money. Dad died last year. I'll prepare a room for you.

–Thank you, Frida. Thank you and forgive me.

–Imbecile...

* * *

AUTHOR'S NOTE *(BONUS TRACK)*

Dear reader. Dear, because you have had the patience and affection to reach this point of my poor document and, therefore, you have earned all my respect and consideration. If you are reading this, you or someone else have invested part of your savings in buying the book, which is something to be thankful for in these times of hardship. Because of this affection, you deserve some extra lines.

The first fear of the author when he or she gets to his keyboard is criticism. This is my case, although I am not a professional author, and I don't mind if my work is branded as this or that. This work reaches your hands because it is the third I have started and the first I have finished, which is reason enough to be happy. The fear of criticism is because, as Leo says, one leaves something of oneself for the whole world to see, and that's quite a commitment.

The other two works were left unfinished because I got bored with the plot and decided that the world already had enough headaches without having to endure another one. Nothing annoys me more than reading something I'm not liking, because I have a hard time letting go of a volume halfway through reading it. In the case of NO-MAD, I had a blast during its development.

Fear of criticism is also because the first thing that came to my mind when I started writing NO-MAD was that it was full of platitudes. Later I discovered that this is precisely what I was looking for: many commonplaces. To be able to talk about things that no one is surprised by. If someone wants to criticize commonplaces, I answer that some hypothetical next novel will be science fiction and full of clichés too! On the other hand, I am interested in knowing the macho man capable of writing a biography of the Cid Campeador without mentioning Rodrigo Díaz de Vivar in a single paragraph.

I wanted to organize a party with no budget limit. I hope that the mayor of Milan will not take it badly, and I also wanted, by mentioning them, to pay my heartfelt tribute to the victims of L'Aquila and do my bit to keep them in the collective memory. Human suffering is always a catastrophe.

I am currently a BI consultant, which I certainly enjoy. Still, BI is not dramatic enough to make a novel protagonist unless you, dear reader, are a fellow professional: data is alive. I like Leo's work somewhat better for these purposes, and it has forced me to study a few things which, since you have been so kind, I will mention briefly.

The protagonist is named Leonardo in honor of his brilliant Renaissance namesake. I think that in the times we live in, the digital revolution is changing many things. The one that strikes me the most is that all the information is available so that learning the data loses meaning in favor of learning the way to look for it: Renaissance 2.0.

Archetypes are a whole world that we humans are still far from fully understanding, but they work very well. In this book, there are many nods to archetypes, and, in all cases, they are the result of careful studies. As a first example, I will tell you that I have been thinking for many years that, thanks to a brand of consoles, we now have more than one generation trained to work with the cross, the circle, the square, and the triangle with the right thumb with the ease with which others snap their fingers. The applications for this training would fill ten books or more. That is the power of archetypes.

The king, the warrior, the magician, and the lover and their female equivalents are also archetypes. You are free to identify which character is performing which task in each moment of NO-MAD. All mythological stories, fables, and children's tales are also archetypal. I didn't get Sandra and Pietro together because it was too obvious to me. Who knows in some possible sequel how their story ends.

Regarding the Nomad Party, I believe that it would be the only party I would take my membership card in this moment of political disbelief. Because I am a mix, and because I believe in integration and in the benefits of non-tourist travel as a way of getting to know and learn from each other.

My experience in writing NO-MAD is the following: you own the first third, and you, dear reader, own the second third. Beyond that, the novel owns itself and writes the ending on its own. I recommend anyone to try the exercise, and I ask those who know how to write to tell me their opinion about it.

The characters are all fictional. Nothing is autobiographical, or almost. The only character named after his alter-ego is Jéjé. Jérôme makes movies, he's a great guy, and he inspired his namesake in NO-MAD. This animal has the lazy laugh of the ferret and the turkey and the tic of the *petit père*. We share quite a few anecdotes, and

I wish we share many more over the years. A hug from here, loco. Thanks for dropping the camera to run the newspaper in the novel.

I would also like to apologize if anyone, because of their nationality, feels biased opinions. Opinions are biased by definition, and there are opinions for all tastes. You can always do like Bismarck, who, as soon as he received an opinion or a piece of advice, gave it to a third party so as not to accumulate garbage, according to his own words.

I thank Robert Graves for his Claudius, which always accompanies me and has given me this ugly writing vice. Also for his other works, citing as the basis of my tireless attempts to understand women, his compilation of poetry called "MAN DOES, WOMAN IS".

If any of my friends or acquaintances feel alluded to or quoted in these heavy lines, I know a few restaurants where I will gladly let them pay the bill. For the rest, I quote Augusto, quoted by Claudio, quoted by Robert, with a: "I lack words, gentlemen. Nothing more I could say could express the depth of my opinion on this matter."

Happy millennium,

Pablo.

Cascais 2010

PS.- I also pay you for your efforts for all the non-English references and save you the search: the Greek word that gives title to the earthquake chapter is "catharsis".

* * *